THE DOOMSAYER QUEEN

WHEEL OF CROWNS BOOK SEVEN

BRANDI ELLEDGE

ALSO BY BRANDI ELLEDGE

ACADEMY OF THE SERAPH:

Blessed

Captured

Broken

THE UNRIVALED SERIES:

House of Deception

House of Agony

WHEEL OF CROWNS SERIES:

The Werewolf Queen

The Queen of Witches

The Vampire Queen

The Demon Queen

The Zombie Queen

The Queen of the Sea

FATED MATES OF NEW ORLEANS:

A Wolf's Craving

A Siren's Calling

A Witch's Curse

A Vampire's Choice

RAVEN ACADEMY SERIES:

Shadow Bringer

Copyright © 2023 by Brandi Elledge

All rights reserved.

No part of this book may be reproduced in any form or by any electronic or mechanical means, including information storage and retrieval systems, without written permission from the author, except for the use of brief quotations in a book review.

This one is for Jersey! I love you BIG. Like super super big.

PROLOGUE

Pressure.

Some of us thrive under it. Others crack.

Of the people who crack, there are two varieties: The ones who can fake it, and the ones who—there's no denying—are having a meltdown.

I always thought I'd be able to fake it. Yes, I might have a couple of small lines running through my foundation, but only if someone looked really closely. I'd never be one of those people who go off the deep end, resembling the chaos before a nuclear bomb. They're screaming, running for their lives with no destination in mind as long as it takes them away from what is coming…what is about to happen.

Turned out I was wrong.

My mother, God rest her soul, cracked under the pressure. It had started with those invisible cracks. No one had seen them. Or if they did, they had seemed so insignificant that no one paid attention until it was too late.

I was following her lead but on a much more unconventional route. I was going out in a blaze of glory. One that I ignited.

Technically this shouldn't have happened to me. My powers were stronger than my mother's were, and what had helped me get this far was the people who surrounded me. They lifted me up…carried me when my legs no longer worked. Without them I had no reason to move forward...to try. So why didn't it end differently for me? I've done the unthinkable. I've messed up. Not the kind of mess up where you leave the milk out of the refrigerator and you have to make a late-night run to the grocery store, but the kind of mess up that brings you to your knees. The kind for which you would sacrifice almost anything to rewind time. The kind of error that, if only you knew then what you know now, it would never have happened.

That's the problem, though. I *did* know. I had a chance to stop the inevitable. Witches cast spells. Vampires use their strength and conniving ways to have other factions bend to their will. Shifters use their animalistic senses to guide them along and they back it up with brute force. Psychics are supposed to see all... know all. Predict the future, and with one fell swoop fix broken timelines. That could cause catastrophic harm. It's my job to know what is coming around the corner, and yet I failed everyone. I have no excuses, and even if I did, how could I look at my loved ones while they were grieving and whisper justifications? They probably blamed me. Of course they blamed me. Who else was at fault?

How would I ever look in my friends' eyes again? My actions brought death to the doorstep of a loved one. Maybe I didn't insert the knife that killed them, but I did worse; I didn't stop the action.

Psychics are funny beings. The burnout is usually evident and imminent unless you can harvest the power you were born with. Let it grow. Manifest. You either embraced it or it killed you. Before the incident, I was losing ground some days, but for the most part I'd learned how to cradle the power that resided inside of me like a newborn baby. It was precious. A gift I wouldn't squander.

Then it all changed. One mistake. One misstep and I no longer cared about harvesting the raging power inside me. I welcomed the burnout and prayed that the flames would take me with it. If I couldn't feel, couldn't think, then the pain would go away. It would be my way of turning back time to when my life was easier.

A time when all I had to worry about was protecting those I

loved. Making sure their timelines were altered for their best outcome. Rewinding the days until all I had to worry about was safeguarding my loved ones and not running from my friends because they could no longer stomach the sight of me.

I'd let my power fizzle. I'd let my light burn out just like it did with my mother. The difference was my mother couldn't control her powers. I could but I was a coward. A quitter that couldn't hold her head up in front of her loved ones. I was changing my fate and praying that soon I wouldn't even remember my name.

CHAPTER 1

Present day...

There were so many voices in my head, all of them trying to talk over one another. They never shut up. Just non-stop jabbering. At some point the voices had become indistinguishable, and I didn't know if that was a blessing or a curse. Eh, who was I kidding? Definitely a curse.

I was pretty sure that I used to have clear pictures of specific things: Ideas, suggestions, or timetables that might help those I love. Then the timelines started zigzagging and crossing over one another. My loved ones' faces fading from memory. I knew that I once had goals. Plans. For the life of me, I couldn't remember those plans anymore.

There was only one thing that I did remember: I was crazy. Mad.

I couldn't let others know it. Of course there was a reason for that, but I couldn't remember the reason. At this point in my life, I was just trying to put the puzzle pieces together, even though I was pretty sure I was working with several different puzzles. Every time I remembered something, I'd hold onto it with both hands and follow the clues. Sometimes what I found at the end of the proverbial road made sense and sometimes it didn't quite connect. On good days, I'd clap myself on the back for getting through another confusing twenty-four hours. On bad days, I wished for an eternal peace that I knew would never be within my reach, at least not if fate had anything to say about it.

I stumbled into a bar, searching for what I didn't know. I pushed my way through the crowd and claimed one of the barstools. My eyes flicked to my image in the long mirror behind the whiskey bottles. Tears filled my eyes as I realized I didn't even recognize myself. Black hair sat on my shoulders. Was it wavy, or just hadn't been brushed and washed in forever? The tips were dyed blue. Who had done that? Both colors—the jet black and cobalt blue—made my dusty skin almost shimmer. My blue eyes might be considered green, and yet there was nothing familiar in them. My lips were almost too big for my pixie face, but it all meshed together well. Who did I take after? Did I have parents? I felt a pang in my heart as if some forgotten memory was trying to tell me the answer to my question.

I looked through the patchwork hobo bag on my shoulder. There was a little bit of money at the bottom. I threw it on the counter and waited for the bartender to pour me something strong. The music was loud. The place was dingy, and I was hoping that the piss-poor lighting would cover the fact that I needed a bath.

I sat there on that stool, waiting for the bartender to notice me.

A male voice that seemed to be on repeat sounded in my head. *"I'm so close to finding the key. I will redeem myself."*

A soft-spoken one said, *"The key. The key. The key!"*

An older voice. The one that was the most persistent. *"Please focus. Steal the key from the witches. Your fate—your well-being depends on it."*

I snorted. Fate was a biatch.

A sexy, deep voice sounded enraged. *"Did the key make it out of the realm? Yes, or no?"*

I banged my head on the sticky bar. Why would they never shut up?

"What will you have?"

My head popped up to look at the bartender. I pushed the cash toward him. "Whatever will buy me four dollars' worth."

"Even disheveled, you are too pretty to be buying your own drinks," the semi-cute bartender said as he threw a dish towel over his shoulder.

The deep sexy voice was back. *"I need an answer."*

I rubbed my forehead. "Oh, someone freaking answer him already."

The bartender gave me a strange look.

"Sorry," I said. "I was talking about the sexy, gravelly voice in my head."

The bartender spun so quickly on his heel that I was surprised his hair stayed in place. He slid a shot of something down the bar to me. Poor guy was probably terrified to come within close proximity of the crazy chick. I saluted him before I flung back the shot. The burn of the cheap whiskey slid down my throat just as the old woman's voice crept back in.

"You must get to the fae land no matter what. If you stay here, you'll die," the elderly one proclaimed.

I groaned out loud. Why were all the voices so morbid? Also, they were the bearers of bad news. Every once in a while I'd like to hear the numbers to a winning lottery ticket. That would be super useful.

I saw someone in my peripheral vision scooting down a seat from me. Whether it was because I smelled funny or because I was talking to myself was anyone's guess.

"You must go." The old woman was tenacious. I'd give her that.

I knew where the old lady wanted me to go, mainly because I had received a vision earlier this morning that left me on the side of the road for at least an hour. I had rolled off the bank and into a drainage ditch. At some point, a mom had come along and pointed me out to her children, making an example out of me. She warned them that drugs were very dangerous and that somewhere a mom was praying for her young, beautiful daughter to come home sober. She never once thought to teach her kids to help a stranger up from a ditch. I guess kindness was overrated when passing judgment.

To her horror, I sat up and flipped her off. I mean, if we were using me as a learning opportunity for her children, we might as well go all in. With one motion, I straightened my shirt and wiped the drool from my chin before asking the kids, "And do you know what that gesture means?"

She had grabbed them both by the arms and ushered them down the sidewalk.

The crown of my head started pounding before I felt a twinge in my temples as the old lady persisted. *Jo, go now!*

"Okay, I'm going."

A man sitting beside me turned toward me. "Who are you talking to, pretty dove?"

I tapped my temple. "It's a little crowded in here."

He misunderstood me. "Do you want me to take you somewhere quieter?"

He was at least twice my age. I rolled my eyes. "Dude, no. Just no."

I stumbled to my feet and to the door. The bouncer who hadn't bothered to card me stood off to the side with a bored look on his face.

I poked him in the side. "Hey, where's the closest mental institution?"

His bushy brows snapped together as he chewed on the toothpick. "Why do you want to know?"

"Cause I'm crazy. Where am I, by the way?" I had a feeling that I was here—wherever here was—for a reason. A vision or a voice must've delivered me here.

He was really staring at me now. "New Jersey. By the sound of your accent, you're a long way from home."

I tried not to sway on my feet as I crossed my arms and stared at him. "Listen, big fella, this is what we're going to do. You're going to call me a taxi and pay for it"—because I had drunk all my money—"and have me delivered to the nearest mental institution, or I'm going to tell the world you gave alcohol to a minor who is mentally unstable." When he just continued to stare at me, I jerked my thumb at my chest. "A daughter of a highly favored politician."

That lie had him moving. He reached into his back pocket and pulled out a cell phone. Within minutes there was a taxi out front. He barked at me, "Don't come back here again."

I waved a hand in the air. "Like I could remember how to get back here to begin with."

I snorted as I crawled into the back of the taxi. I couldn't remember my name at the moment, and until I saw myself in the mirror a few minutes ago, I didn't know what I looked like.

My nose started dripping blood as a vision came to me. It was one I was certain I'd seen before. A girl named Madeline sat huddled in a medical bed. She was the soft voice from earlier. She could see glimpses of the future. She wasn't powerful by any means, but she saw enough to make her crazy. Her mind had cracked, and she couldn't bounce back. Her sisters—who were part of a witch's coven—left her behind because they thought she was dead weight. With her constant ramblings she was bringing nothing to the table. Obviously they felt no familial obligations to her, and some good Samaritan helped Madeline get placed in a mental institution. The elderly gentleman had found her living behind a dumpster, confused and incoherent.

Madeline was a good apple in a rotten apple farm. In a saner moment, she took an important key and hid it from her sisters. The witches were convinced that the demons that they stole the key from had stolen it back while they were sleeping.

Joke's on them. That's what they get for dumping their sister off in the streets.

Fifteen minutes later, the taxi driver said softly, "The bar has already paid me, so you are good to go. Do you need help to the door?"

That had me tearing up. I was a mess. "No, sweetness. I got this. Thanks, though."

Shoulders squared and head back, I marched up to the brick building that looked as old as I felt. I might be eighteen, but on the inside, I felt closer to two hundred. I was tired. Something had to give, or I'd end up like Madeline. Maybe this was my last lap. At least I could rest then.

I hit the buzzer and waited patiently for the double doors to open. After being admitted into the entrance, I headed to what looked like a front desk.

A plump woman with frizzy red hair and way too much makeup asked, "Can I help you?"

"I'd like to visit Madeline Carmichael."

"Oh, visiting hours are over." She gave me a narrowed look. "And if you are friends with Ms. Carmichael, I assume you know that she's not feeling her best right now. We can't afford to bring her any undue stress. You'll have to come back tomorrow, though I'm not promising the doctor will allow visitors even during normal visiting hours."

I winced as I heard the old woman's voice in my head. "No time. Act now."

"Are you okay?" the receptionist asked.

"No. No, I'm not. I hear voices all the time. They won't stop. I need to be evaluated and medicated, and probably not in that order. Also, don't ask me to fill out paperwork. I can't remember my name, much less my address."

Welp, that's all it took. With one push of her finger, two buff-looking guys came over and not so gently escorted me into a smaller room. And that is how one finds themselves institutionalized.

∼

Visions were pounding in my head as I was led to an evaluating room. I snagged one of the nurse's keycards and put it in my back pocket while I pretended to trip over my own feet. They sat me down on an examining table while they explained the evaluation process. My nose started to bleed, and I grew nauseated as the visions were rammed into my head.

Madeline's sisters were at the nearby zoo. They were summoning a demon, and because they knew his name, they would be in complete control of him. It wasn't going to go as planned, though. They were going to torture a nice demon. There were nice demons? They can't find the key. They had no clue it was actually Madeline who had it. They were going to try to command the demon to take down the Demon Queen.

A memory fizzed at the back of my mind. Did I know the Demon Queen? With that last thought, I threw up all over the nice nurse standing in front of me. There was a moment of shock on her face before she took several steps back.

The nurse on her right sighed and said, "Some got on my shoes." Then he took a few steps back as well. "We're going to get cleaned up." He put a waste bin under me. "Just in case you have another accident. We will be right back."

As soon as the door shut, I got up and used one of the nurse's cards to unlock the door. Letting myself out, I went through a maze of hallways that I knew from the visions. I found Madeline in a sterile room. Her limp, blonde hair lay fanned out on the pillow. Her body looked frail in the bright lights. Her eyes were glassy, and she didn't notice me.

Today, I was the one coming to her. But soon enough, this would be me, dying in a bed alone. Would anyone come? Did I have someone who cared for me? Or would I lie here, spent until there was nothing left of me, no one to remember me? Sadness and desperation crept into me like a disease spreading through all my veins. I didn't want to lie here like Madeline one day, but I was also exhausted just like the broken girl before me. My path, like hers, felt inevitable.

I slid my hand under the mattress and snagged the eight-ball, torn between escaping what might soon be my future and helping to ease her passage to the next world.

Tired eyes flicked to mine. "Can I rest now?"

I laid my hand on top of hers. "You've done well. Go rest."

A smile lit her face a moment before the sound of a machine beside her bed announced that Madeline's time here was done. I wanted to cry for the girl I only knew through visions, but there wasn't time. Never enough time. With the sound of shoes hitting the floor, I made my escape during the chaos.

CHAPTER 2

I should have gone home, but I couldn't remember where home was. I stood outside the mental hospital and wondered where I could go without money. There was little doubt that I, too, would end up like Madeline. In the end, she welcomed death. I had a feeling that I would also. She ended up with no family surrounding her. No one to tell her that they loved her or would miss her.

It was her family who put her in the facility, knowing that she was going to break soon. I knew the witches were meeting ten miles from here in a zoo. I could find a bench to sleep on and wait for a vision to tell me where I was needed next, or I could go fight Madeline's battle for her since she was no longer here to do it herself.

I hefted my heavy purse onto my shoulder and started speed walking to my destination. Two hours and twenty minutes later, I arrived at the zoo. I didn't have calories to burn but I was a woman on a mission. I climbed a short wall, precariously balancing on the ledge. I then jumped to a higher wall. It took me what seemed like ages to pull myself up and over. Jeez, I needed to join a weightlifting class. Not that I would remember to show up. I dropped twenty feet to the ground and felt a jarring pain all the way up my shins. At least I was on a walkway and not in the lion's den. According to my vision, I needed to be at the panther containment right before midnight. I looked down at my watch and discovered it was broken. Huh? When did that happen?

Plan B, I would wait until they summoned their demon and then I would make a deal with said demon.

"Need to get to the fae world," the old lady insisted.

"Shh," I said out loud, making a bird flap its wings in a nearby cage. "First I avenge Madeline, and then I'll go to your fae world."

How does one even get to the fae world? I'm pretty sure you can't just call an Uber.

A sexy, deep voice said, *"The demons lost the key to witches? It's only a matter of time before the Winter King finds it again. We can't let that happen."*

When did keys become the new Pokémon?

I neared the panther sanctuary. Five witches encircled some sort of containment symbol drawn on the ground. In the middle of their drawing lay a black panther. Poor baby had been shot with a tranquilizer gun. It took everything I had to stand there and bide my time.

Their arms were stretched out wide, and their heads were thrown back. I couldn't hear them from here, but their mouths were moving. The door was unlocked, so I quietly opened it and tiptoed my way to a nearby tree. Leaning up against it, I waited. The leader called forth her demon and I bit back a smile. This wasn't going to go the way she wanted it to.

Black smoke curled around the body of the panther before disappearing into it. The dart pushed its way out of the rear quarter, and then moments later the beast made its way to his feet. The panther slowly took in his surroundings. His dark eyes drifted over to me, and I gave him a little finger wave.

The leader said, "Faimah, we command you to do our bidding."

The panther sat in the circle and began to lick himself.

One of the witches looked at the leader. "Why isn't it working?"

I stepped from the shadows of the tree. "Evening, ladies."

They all gasped and spun toward me.

"You see, you didn't originally say 'Faimah,' and you've called forward the wrong demon."

The leader shook her head. "No, I said Faimah."

"But, you didn't," I replied. My eyes went to the panther then back to them. They all stood there with their mouths slightly agape. I gave them an overbright smile that really complimented my crazy. "Oh, hey! Sorry, I'm sure you're confused as to who I am, but I can't answer that because I have no clue." I giggled, making them take a step back. Yep, everyone feared crazy. "So, um…I'm here to tell you that your sister died tonight."

One of them narrowed her eyes on me. "Madeline?"

"I'm glad you could remember her name since you basically threw her to the wolves." My anger made my voice turn sharp. "She couldn't remember your faces in the end. She couldn't even remember her own, and you just gave her a wad of cash and dropped her off on a busy street."

She half-growled. "You should have minded your business."

I tilted my head back and laughed, showing my full crazy.

"Sweetie, if I could mind my business, I would."

She took a step toward me. "Unless you have useful information like what this demon's name is, I suggest you leave before you regret it."

Twin blue flames erupted from her hands. I tilted my head to the side. "Don't mean to interrupt the light show but quick question, can you kill a demon with fire, considering they are made from brimstone?"

"Are you stupid? The fire is for you, not the demon."

"Not stupid. Just crazy. But now that we have all of that worked out…" I once again looked at the panther. "Fatimah with a T." I giggled. "And she called me stupid? Anywho, I release you from your circle, and I command you to chase these witches from the premises. You can eat them if you want."

Knowing that a burst of fire would be headed my way soon, I sat abruptly on the grass as flames shot over my head and slammed into the rock enclosure. I spent the next twenty minutes watching the mayhem. Fatimah took a few bites out of witches, and I cheered him on with enthusiasm. For a demon trapped in a panther's body, he was really working his new form. I watched as the wounded and bleeding witches ran from the enclosure in a desperate attempt to escape. I heard the sound of a lock and sighed. Silly witches.

The panther strolled over to me.

"So, that was entertaining," I said. "Do you need help getting back to where you're from?"

The panther came right up to my face, sniffed me, and then purred. "Baby, home is where the heart is, and I think you own my heart."

I patted his big head. "That's cute, but unnecessary. Are you ready to go?"

Before he could reply, a vision came to me. I was at a hotel in New Jersey. There were demons planning on attacking a fae girl in a hotel room. I needed to be there to rescue her. It was part of my destiny, but honestly, at this point, did I want to keep chasing after visions? More images flickered through my head before finally a calming peace settled over me.

As the vision faded, the old woman in my head quietly said, *"Your fae prince is your mate. He will help you find your way back. You need to heal."*

Way back to where?

"Whoa," Fatimah said, "You're bleeding, precious."

I wiped my nose. "Yeah, I get visions. When I've had too many in a day, I get nose bleeds—or at least I think I do. I mean, that sounds right."

He cocked his head to the side.

I continued on, "I also hear voices and I can't remember anything anymore. I'm pretty sure I'm dying."

I needed more sleep than normal, and there was a huge problem with that. I was so far gone that sleep didn't heal me. In fact, every time I went to sleep, I lost a memory. Another name, another face of a loved one gone forever. It was just a matter of time before I was lying in a hospital bed like Madeline. Sadness washed over me.

The panther showed all his teeth. Either that was his attempt at a smile, or he was about to eat me.

"Then you need me," he said.

I shook my head. "I can't have a pet demon."

"Why?"

Hell if I knew, but it didn't sound right. "I'll probably forget to feed you, and then you'll be forced to eat people."

He nodded his massive head. "Population control, baby."

"I don't know if I have the emotional capacity to care. Honestly, people suck." My forehead wrinkled. "I might be a villain. Villains would definitely have a pet demon."

"Of course they do!" The panther flicked his tail. "I could come in handy. You said you can't remember anything. Maybe I could remember things for you?"

That actually wasn't a bad idea. "All right, but I have to tell you right now that you better not throw up hairballs on my boots," I said as I stood up. "Here's your first assignment: I need you to remember that before Wednesday night—specifically at midnight—I need to get to a hotel in New Jersey. The one with a casino that's close to the shore. I also need you to remember that the fae prince is my mate. Oh, and that I need to rescue a pretty brunette fae. If we arrive on schedule, then she'll be in the downstairs lobby bathroom before she goes up to her room."

The panther pushed his gigantic head against my thigh. "You got it."

"If you don't remind me, I'll have to fire you."

He trotted to the door. "Yeah, but I'll probably forget to tell you to fire me."

"Touché." I pointed at the door. "Now unlock the door."

He narrowed his eyes. "How did you know that I could unlock doors?"

I smiled, showing my crazy. "I saw it in that vision. Along with you stealing a car for us."

If a panther could look pouty, he did. "If you knew I was going with you, why did you act like it was a bad idea?"

I shrugged. "I'm crazy. I don't have to explain myself. That's the only joy I have left."

"Doll face, you are completely nuts, and I'm here for it."

And that is how I found myself riding down the highway with a new partner in crime. Sometimes life throws you curveballs, and sometimes it throws you demons.

CHAPTER 3

"So, recap," I said, "You don't know my name, but you call me Nuts, and I get visions because I'm psychic. The visions are making me crazy, but you like crazy."

The panther swung his massive head toward me. "Yep. I'm your best friend."

I narrowed my eyes. "And why should I trust you?"

"Well, because you're crazy, and trusting a talking panther is definitely something that a crazy person would do. Or at least manifest in their head."

I sat in the middle of a deserted field. His words weren't entirely off-putting, and it did semi-explain the voices I kept hearing. "That's fair."

"Also, you told me on the long drive here that you think a fae prince is going to quiet the voices for you and make you better, so I'm ninety-nine percent sure that you're slowly dying from your power."

"That sucks."

He flicked his tail. "Yeah."

"So why am I here?"

"Not sure. We've been together for two days, and so far, all I can tell is once you fall asleep, even if it's a power nap, you forget everything. And I mean *everything*." A homeless man started venturing our way and the panther let out a low growl, making the man wobble on his feet before he ran from us.

"So, you don't know why we are sitting in a park at night."

He curled into a tiny ball, looking so cute. "Oh, actually I do know that. It's because I'm a panther and we've been chased from every establishment in the area. The cops may be looking for you as we speak. You made the news. Beside the fact that you are a celebrity, in a more lucid moment you said you needed to get to the casino because that's where your destiny is."

"Do I have a gambling problem?"

"One can hope, but that's not what you told me. You said you needed to rescue a pretty fae girl with brown hair. She'll be in the lobby bathroom when we arrive before midnight."

"That's specific and yet not helpful all at the same time." I rubbed a hand down my dirty face. "How am I going to get into the casino?"

He lifted one massive paw and swiped at a bag on my shoulder. "I don't know, Nuts. I mean, you're broke. As in *no dinero*."

I looked at the purse lying next to me. "I have no money?"

He shook his head.

"I'm crazy and can't remember anything. I'm friends with a talking panther and I'm broke. This is horrible."

"I'm actually a demon in a panther's body, but semantics." He let out a loud yawn. "Hurry so I can get some good shut-eye."

"How exactly are you going to find me?"

"You're my master. I'll find you wherever you go."

Well, that wasn't creepy at all.

An old lady protruded into my thoughts. *Jo, please go to the casino. Your fate awaits you there.*

I pressed my palms into my temples. This was no way to live. Standing on shaky legs, I walked across the grass to the big building covered in neon signs.

"I'll see you soon," the panther called. "We can watch a fun movie tonight."

I didn't turn back. "Yeah. Sure."

I stepped out into the road without looking, and a car horn sounded. I waved a hand, apologizing as I ran across the road toward the massive hotel. I followed the signs pointing to the casino, but stopped and contemplated my next move as people streamed around me. Where exactly was I supposed to go?

The old lady sounded in my head. *"Bathroom. Last stall. Hurry."*

"What are you talking about, old woman?"

She sighed. *"Rescue the fae girl. She'll be in the last stall. It will help you. Don't tell anyone about the key."*

How can you tell someone about something that you don't even remember?

I made my way to the bathroom and groaned when I saw there was a long line. The three girls in front of me turned toward me with a look of horror. I quickly took in their appearance. Nice dresses, even nicer shoes, makeup and hair done to perfection. Then I scanned myself. I was wearing dirty clothes covered in grass stains, and I was pretty sure that the stench I smelled was coming from me.

The blonde with over-tweezed eyebrows said, "Rough day, sweetie?"

I lifted a shoulder. "For all I know, it's been a rough year. A voice in my head told me to stop by the bathroom."

The short redhead nodded. "Hey, when you have to go, you have to go."

The brunette was giving me a condescending look. She elbowed the blonde and whispered, "She looks crazy. Don't talk to her."

The blonde shushed her friend and turned to me apologetically.

I held up a hand. "To be fair, your friend is probably accurate. I mean I did listen to a talking panther who thinks he's a demon. He recently told me that I'm going to meet my prince—who is fae, by the way—and some lady in my head told me that I need to rescue a girl in the last stall, so here I am."

And just like that, all three girls hopped out of the line. I scooted up as they quickly made their escape. Ten grueling minutes later, I was in the bathroom waiting for the last stall door to open. When it did, a frumpy middle-aged woman came out. I was just about to explain to her that demons were on their way to kill her when all of a sudden, a brunette asked me if I was waiting for the bathroom. I told her to go ahead with a smile. She must be the fae that I had to speak to.

I stood there patiently, waiting for the girl to exit. It wasn't until she had washed her hands and was leaving the bathroom that she noticed me following her. She sped up as she walked down the long hall, looking over her shoulder.

Finally, she whirled around on me. "Are you following me?"

"Yes. Glad you noticed. It's always good to check your surroundings."

Her hand flew to her throat. Her fingers grabbed a small necklace as she looked around wildly. "Who are you?"

"Um...Nuts?"

"You're crazy?"

"Well, yes, but it's not nice to point it out. My demon cat calls me Nuts. Just to clarify."

Her big, brown eyes widened as she took a step back from me. "Why are you following me?"

"Because a voice in my head told me to."

She took another step away from me and clutched her purse in front of her.

I rolled my eyes so hard I felt something behind my corneas snap. As she was planning on making her getaway, a few images flitted to me. "Okay, you had a pet when you were three that looked like a tiny dragon. It was pink. Your father killed it to teach you a life lesson. By the way, he's a total bag of male anatomy. Your second oldest brother is your favorite person in the world. You think he hung the moon and the stars. You came here to track down some demons. You've been here for almost two days, and you're worried that one of the guards from the winter court will see you and know that you are looking for the demons. Spoiler: No one will see you as long as you leave tonight. I'm sure there have been other things that I've seen, but I forget things fast."

She took in my appearance and then said, "You hear voices, and you see things. You're a very powerful psychic."

I shrugged.

She gave me a funny look. "I can tell when someone is lying. Most fae can."

I actually didn't. Or if I did, I had long forgotten about it.

"Why are you here?" she asked.

"It's part of my destiny."

She raised her eyebrows like she was waiting for me to elaborate.

I said, "The demons don't have what you are looking for. However, you were spying on them when they lost it. They caught your scent about an hour ago. They think you have it." I lowered my voice, "A witch had it, though. They are on the wrong path. Sucks for them. Anyway, they plan on trapping you and taking you back to the winter court. There will be torture sessions and"—I wrinkled my nose—"a ton of blood."

"Will they find me?" she asked with horror.

"Not if you hurry."

Without hesitation she snagged my hand. "Come with me."

We were practically running down the hall, causing people to stare at us. Or it could have been my over-bright smile that had them glancing our way. I followed the woman onto an elevator up ten stories before she got off and took a card from her back pocket, opening up a door.

She went into the room and grabbed a bag. "I can't leave any sign that I've been here." She threw some items into it. "Do you want to come with me? The fae courts have natural healing magic in the air. It might not cure you, but it would stop you from worsening."

I shook my head. "No, I think I'm supposed to wait here for someone."

At that moment, voices trickled in, all talking over one another. So many. I bent over and winced. I lost track of time, but when I was finally able to stand upright, the pretty girl had a wet washcloth on the back of my neck and was sitting beside me on the edge of the bed.

"You poor thing. I shouldn't say this, but I know someone that could help with this problem."

My eyes jerked to her as my stomach roiled again. "Problem?"

She nodded. Her dark brown eyes took in my face with a look of worry. "They could help the madness."

"Madness" was a nice way of describing how I felt. There was a shout at the door.

"Nuts, let me in!"

I rushed to the door and opened it as the panther burst through. He took one look at the brunette and said, "Hello, sweetness, are you my treat for being a good kitty?"

She arched one brow. "So, this is your panther?"

I nodded.

"He's a demon," she said.

"So, I've been told."

She emptied a drawer and then put her heavy bag on her shoulder. "Interesting."

The panther pranced by her before turning and prancing the other way. "I'm helping her with her short-term memory problem. I'm like a walking journal. But I could be more for you."

She wrinkled her nose. "I think I'll pass." Her brown eyes looked at me again. "This voice you heard telling you to help me, who is it?"

I shrugged, but the panther said, "Her name is Ariana, and she helps Nuts sometimes."

"I'm Vanka and I really hate to run, but apparently there are demons chasing me. I do feel like I owe you though."

It took me a second to realize that she was talking to me. "Oh…no, I'm good."

"Actually, sweetness," the panther said, "Can we have the room?"

"Sure," she answered. "It's all yours. Checkout is at eleven tomorrow." She walked to the door. "Are you sure I can't convince you to come with me? I really do think you could get help with your, um…"

"Insanity?" the panther said.

She bit her lip before she nodded.

I waved a hand. "No, really, it's okay. I'm supposed to be here at this casino for a reason."

The panther said, "What if she's the reason?"

I didn't think so, but hadn't my demon said something about my destiny and a fae prince?

"Can I ask you a question," Vanka said, "Do the demons find the key?"

Oh this one was an easy one. I actually knew the answer to this one. Yay, me.

"No."

I stopped Vanka before she could open the door. "One thing, though?"

She turned to look at me. "Yes?"

"The bar…can we charge it to your room?"

She laughed a musical sound. She put one hand over her heart. "Of course. And do yourself a favor…" Her eyes darted to the panther, who was licking himself. "Try to give yourself time to heal in between the voices and visions."

The panther brushed up against my hand. "Yeah, except for me. Tell me everything, bestie."

That earned the panther a smile from the beautiful fae. "Thank you for being a good friend to her."

The voices were crowding in again. I tried so hard to keep them at bay, but they were persistent. One demonic voice said, "Tenth floor. I can smell Fatimah and Vanka."

I stumbled back. "Who is Fatimah?"

The panther's head swung up to look at me. "Me."

"There are five demons headed here now, and I think they can smell you both." I shoved Vanka out the door. "You have to hurry."

She wrinkled her brow. "I thought you said I had time?"

"Well yeah, but that's because I saw me pushing you out of the room. Now hurry."

She hesitated, but the panther growled at her, getting her to jump before she gave him a weary smile. "Okay, okay, I'm going. I won't forget this, Nuts. Maybe I can return the favor one day."

As soon as I shut the door, I smiled at Fatimah. "She was the nicest spy I've ever talked with."

"Spy? For whom?" The panther shook his head. "Never mind. So, I put a fancy blade in your purse. You might want to grab it."

I blinked several times. "And do what with it?"

"Duh! Try to cut them with it."

"Are you crazy?" I half shouted.

He laughed. "Oh, that's rich. And no, I'm not. Listen, Nuts, when you get really stressed you do some pretty crazy things. You're more than just a psychic, but I'm not sure what exactly. You look like a vampire, but you don't have fangs. You chant like a witch, smell like a fae, have the craziness of a shifter that can't shift, and you move in darkness like a demon."

"Define 'crazy things,'" I said while getting the dagger out of my purse. "What exactly do I do?"

"Some random guy one night was trying to hurt a child and you disappeared like poof. The guy screamed. The kid got away, and when you reappeared, you had blood on your hands and were wearing a crazy smile that made me fall in love even more."

"You think I killed some guy?"

His ears twitched, and he cocked his head to the side. "They're almost here. Let's hope I'm right, Nuts."

I snorted. Hope was a funny thing.

Forty-five seconds later, there was a knock, and I watched in fascination as Fatimah hit the door handle and let in five large demons. Talk about making it easy for them. A demon tried to grab me as another went after my cat. The last thing I remembered was my chuckling.

CHAPTER 4

THERE WAS AN EMPTY BOTTLE LYING SIDEWAYS ON AN OLD DRESSER. The remainder of the contents had made a mess on the furniture and the floor below, but that wasn't the most concerning thing. I had lost my marbles. Insane. Bat shit crazy. And yet my insanity still wasn't the most distressing thing in the room. Nope. It was the five dead demons haphazardly laying in my hotel room.

I slowly sat up and removed a limb that was draped over my legs.

"Sorry," I whispered to the dead demon. He didn't seem to mind. I rubbed my temples as the smell of rum wafted from my pores.

"Ouch," I said to my unlively audience. I shifted to my left and reached underneath me. My brows snapped together. I had been laying on what looked like an eight-ball. Had we been shooting pool? I looked around again at the dead demons. I was highly competitive, but even this was a little much for me.

A familiar voice started slashing its way through my mind, but I couldn't remember the person's name. *"You must go with him. You should have already left but you are always shutting me out."*

I groaned. "This again? Why am I always going? What's up with all these dead demons? Why do I smell of stale cigarettes?"

"Child, hush! Listen to me...develop a connection. Don't fight the

spark. He could be your salvation. Your mate will save you if you just let him."

"This is really bad timing. Could you check back in when I'm not lying in the middle of a pile of dead bodies?"

"You should have gone with the fae woman, Vanka. That's why I sent you there," the old woman said.

"Who?" I rubbed my eyes with the heels of my hand, trying to get the grit out.

The old lady sighed. *"Since you can't remember how to get yourself there, unfortunately you only have one more opportunity. You must go with the prince."*

"Listen, listen, listen. Go, go, go. Well let me tell you something, my ears are tired, and I don't have a good pair of walking shoes. I'm exhausted from all the listening and going. I need rest."

Her voice boomed in my head. *"You will get eternal rest if you do not heed my advice."*

"I'd take any kind of rest at this point."

Her voice quieted, and I was certain that I had made the old woman mad. Good. I didn't care and I wouldn't remember that I had offended anyone tomorrow, so win-win.

I'd barely made it to my feet when the door opened. A handsome man came into the room. His blue eyes swept over the carnage before they snapped to me.

I straightened my T-shirt that read, "My own sugar mama," and wiped my hands on my leather pants.

"Are you with hotel management?"

He stared at me without blinking.

"So, I'm pretty sure the hotel chain has insurance for stuff like this."

He cocked his head to the side. "Are you talking about the rum that has spilled all over the floor or the dead demons that are piled up beside it?"

I held up a finger. "First of all, not all the rum was spilled. I mean, I do smell like a mill, so some must've made it to my tummy. Secondly, the demons aren't really piled upon one another. They are kind of spaced about evenly."

He came into the room, letting the door shut behind him. A look of menace crossed his handsome face. This is probably where I should be running, but I was too tired. I yawned as he looked around the room, his hands in his pockets as he stepped over the fallen demons. He took in everything, silently calculating. His eyes flickered to my wrist and narrowed. I looked down to see a hospital band. I must've had a fun night.

"Are you going to kill me?" I asked nonchalantly, almost wishing he would. I was tired. Bone weary, exhausted, and losing any will to keep going.

"I hadn't planned on it."

The room spun and my head started pounding as a vision came to me. This man was looking for something that looked like the eight-ball I had been lying on. He needed it. He called it something...and it was important for him to have it. I hid the ball behind me as visions of other similar objects pushed into my brain. Flashes were coming to me as a warm hand grabbed my elbow. I blinked open my eyes as blood hit the carpet.

"Your nose is bleeding," he said.

"Yep. I see that." My eyes jerked to where his hand lay on my arm. Just with the touch of his hand, he had made the voices and images stop.

"I'll go get you a washcloth. Don't move."

"Hmm," I said as he stepped away. My eyes darted around the room, landing on a purse. I jumped over a tangle of legs and snagged the bag, stuffing the black object inside it. I had put the bag on my shoulder just as the fae came back into the room.

His eyes landed on my purse. "Are you planning on leaving?"

I shrugged. "It kind of looks like the party is over."

He walked over to me without once looking down. I winced when he stepped on a demon's hand. He put the cloth up to my nose and held it there.

"Why do you get nosebleeds?"

"People won't stop talking to me."

He nodded as if that made complete sense. "Were these demons talking too much?"

I lifted one shoulder. "Honestly, I don't remember."

Again he nodded as if he understood. I was glad one of us did. I must have blacked out. That seemed to be happening more and more recently.

"I have been following these demons for a while. They had some information regarding a key. Do you know where the key is?" He was talking slowly as if he thought I couldn't process the words coming out of his mouth.

"Nope."

"Did they mention the key?"

I pushed his hand away. "Dude, honestly, I don't remember them." I tapped my finger on my head. "I have issues."

Again with the head nod. It was one thing to admit that you were crazy, but it was another thing to have someone agree with you.

He sighed as if he were trying not to lose his patience. "I think if you had seen the key, you would remember."

"Cool. So, this has been a fun and interesting morning that I probably won't remember, but I really need to be going now."

He arched his brow. "To where?"

"Ireland."

The corner of his mouth tilted up. "You don't have plans to go to Ireland."

I crossed my arms. "How would you know, weirdo?"

"I can tell when someone is lying."

I scrunched up my face. "Well, that's off-putting."

He tilted his head to the side. "What's your name, creature?"

I didn't answer him because I didn't know.

He pinched the bridge of his nose. "Nothing concerning the key is ever easy."

This time I nodded. Let's see how he likes it.

"You are mentally unstable?"

"Well, I don't like to put labels to my flaws, but sure, if you want to be crass, I guess you could say that."

"You don't know how these demons ended up like this?"

"Actually, I am recalling something," I said excitedly. It was always a blessing when a memory flashed before me. "There was a busy street, and I was in an old car that had money in the trunk. My brother and I climbed out of the car and told my friends that if we weren't out in fifteen minutes, something was wrong."

"Out from where?"

"I guess this hotel. We went up several flights of steps. By 'we,'

I mean my brother and me. We were discreetly looking around because, you know, super shady area."

The fae male looked confused. "This area?"

"Duh. Anyway, we knocked on a door and this Spanish-speaking man opened the door with an easy smile, but plot twist: He wasn't a real friend."

"The Spanish-speaking guy?"

I rolled my eyes. "Sí. Hello, aren't you listening? Also, I usually have a Spanish accent. I have zero clue why I sound so southern. I digress. So, the guy asked me if I had the money, and I said no, but I did because it was in the trunk. Then I asked him if he had my stuff."

"Please tell me you're not talking about drugs."

"Things got heated and there were guns everywhere. They threatened my brother. Then they brought out a chainsaw."

He raised a brow. "A chainsaw?"

"Yeah, it was a bloody mess. Did not enjoy it. Zero stars. The good news is my friends burst through the door with their guns and rescued me. Of course, it was too late for my brother." I rubbed my temples. "You should never bring a chainsaw to a gunfight."

At that time, a black panther came striding around the corner. The fae jumped and then angled himself in a funny crouching position.

"Demon," he hissed as his hands lit with a blue fire. "I'll send you back to the depths of hell."

The beautiful black panther flicked his tail before he said, "You could, but once Nuts witnesses you killing me, she will more than likely kill you. She's kind of attached to me."

"Who the hell is Nuts?" the fae asked, and I was glad. This whole situation was getting confusing.

"The dollface behind you."

The fae looked at me for confirmation, and I just shrugged.

"Also," the panther said to me, "You don't have a brother, nor a Spanish accent." The panther sat down, not at all concerned with the cute fae who was holding a significant amount of magic in his hands. "You are literally reciting a scene from *Scarface*."

I slowly nodded. "Well, that makes sense." At least for my life.

The fae snuffed out the magic in his hands before he said in an exaggerated tone, "No. No, it does not. Nothing yet has made sense."

I patted his back because I felt sorry for him. "I feel this way all the time. I joined a group."

The panther shook his head. "She didn't." His feline orbs swung my way. "Also, I'd like the record to show that I don't like this guy. He has a car-salesman look to him."

The fae moved with speed as he grabbed the panther by his neck and held him against the wall. I put both hands over my racing heart before I screamed, "I will call the animal activists right now if you don't put the pretty kitty down!"

"Demon," the fae said, "tell me right now what the hell is going on or I'll send you back to the darkness from which you crawled from."

"Okay," the panther wheezed. "Jeez. I'll tell you but put me down first."

As soon as the panther was released, he sat on his haunches and started licking his fur. "Gross. That's all I need is to be smelling like pretty boy fae. Yuck."

The fae growled.

The panther said, "All right give me a second." After his tongue swiped his fur one more time, he said, "So these nasty witches opened up a portal to summon a high-level demon to do their bidding."

I clapped my hands as I walked around a dead demon. "Story time!" I sat down in the only clean spot in the room and began to scratch the panther behind the ears. "Tell me all about them nasty witches."

"They had stolen a key from a group of demons but then lost it literally the same day. Talk about bad luck. Anyway, they wanted to summon a demon to get help tracking the other demons. Really it was a bad idea, but you know how witches can be."

"Totally," I lied.

The panther purred. "Well, they weren't as smart as they thought they were because they um...well, they—"

"They called a low-level demon," the fae said with a dry tone.

"Shut your face, pretty boy," I spat at the fae before turning to the panther. "Ignore him. Tell Mama the rest of the story."

"Well, they did their ceremony at the zoo. I didn't get a human body, but I got this form instead."

I scratched between his ears. "Super cool, by the way. I mean, who doesn't want to be a panther?"

He seemed to preen at my words. "Gorgeous here was in the zoo, just waiting to show those witches what was up."

"I was?"

The panther nodded. "Yep. You released me and commanded me to chase them because you are an evil queen without a crown. Which works for me. Apparently, I like crazy chicks because I'm not going back to serve my demon lord. I'm staying with Nuts. Besides, she needs me."

I put his massive head between my hands and kissed him on the nose. "That's so cute."

"I can't believe you just kissed a demon," the fae male said with enough disgust that had me glaring. "Where is this key at?"

The panther said, "Who knows. Maybe the witches have it by now."

The fae looked at me and then back at the demon. "And what is wrong with her?"

"Too many visions. It's made her a tad on the crazy side."

I watched the fae male as he began to move around the room, searching the dead demons' pockets.

This room was overcrowded with the dead demon bodies. I should go, but to where? And did I get to keep the panther? I don't recall if I had always been an animal lover or not, but finders keepers.

I opened my bag, making sure that the fae couldn't see inside. There was no wallet. Instead, I found tickets to a band I had never heard of, a banana, and a hood ornament. In the zipper pocket there was a nurse's badge with a photo ID. Apparently Pamela was a caretaker at Grand Meadow Sanatorium. Considering the mess, I was currently in, I'm assuming I was in a ward. Poor Pam, she didn't know what she had gotten herself into when she decided to sign up to take care of this hot mess express.

Without looking at me, the fae asked, "Did you find anything interesting?"

"Meh," I said. "So, I'm just going to head out. I think I'll take the panther with me."

I made my way to the door, the panther purring loudly at my side, just as the door faded to a gazebo and the once stale and corpse-holding room I had been in faded to a beautiful garden.

The fae appeared at my elbow. "Wait, lovely."

I narrowed my eyes on him. "Oh, that's funny. Cast your illusions on the chick that you think is mentally ill."

"You see through my illusions?"

I looked over at the panther. He was swatting at a butterfly that wasn't really there. Hands on hips, I faced the fae. "I might be insane but I'm not stupid."

His brows furrowed. "You're very powerful."

He was studying me long and hard, which I didn't mind because my brain was being hammered with a vision. My eyes glazed over while images flashed before me. The pounding in my head made me nauseous as I silently begged for the pain to ease. When the vision was done being shoved into my frontal lobe, the world stopped spinning.

He started to reach out and touch me but then dropped his hand back to his side. "Do you know what I am?"

"Dead man walking."

He leaned forward with a look of confusion on his angelic face. "I'm sorry, what do you mean?"

"I mean that when you leave here, you're going to go through the front door. Bad move. There are three shifters waiting on you. They will take you by surprise. They will throw an iron net over you, and you will become as weak as the day you were born. They will take you to their holding in the mountains, where they will torture you for information about the key you are looking for. You won't give them any info, not because you are stubborn but because you don't know the location of the key. You'll eventually escape but it'll take ten years." I yawned. "I'm hungry."

He was back to staring at me weirdly. "You're a very powerful psychic."

I shrugged. "Guess that would explain all the weird visions

I've been receiving." I turned to the panther. "How does this work? Do we charge him?" I looked back at the fae. "How much is ten years of your life worth?"

The panther said, "I told you we should get a Venmo account."

Ignoring us both, the fae said, "Without proper guidance you are probably burning out." He reached out and snagged my elbow. The voices immediately quietened. There was always chatter, but when he touched me, I heard nothing. Blissful silence surrounded me. I wanted to step toward him, lay my head on his chest, and purr like a kitten, but that would probably be weird. Weird is probably what got me in the mental institution.

The panther pushed in between us. "Whoa, whoa, whoa. What is happening?"

With wide eyes I stared at the panther. "I can't hear anything."

The panther repeated himself with careful enunciation. "WHAT IS HAPPENING?"

"All the voices are hushed," I said in awe.

They were both ignoring me as they talked over me.

The fae male said, "I'm taking this woman to my realm. I can help her, and with her gift, I think she can help me."

"You mean you are going to use her," the panther replied.

"We are going to help each other. I will help her to keep whatever little bit of her sanity she has left as long as she helps me look for the key."

I looked at his hand that was still on my elbow. This was the first time in a long time I felt like I could focus for a second. Maybe I should go with him? In reality, I'd be using him.

The panther looked at me. "Your call, dollface."

I shrugged one shoulder. "I don't really have any plans, do you?"

The fae gave me a look like he was about to show us more of that blue fire. His jaw clenched, and his expression changed. "The demon is not coming."

"Listen, buddy," I said, "we are a package deal. If you need my help, you have to take the panther as well."

Talking through his teeth he said, "I cannot take a demon to my realm."

I just stared at him.

"Would you prefer that I kill you both here and now?" he asked.

I rolled my eyes. He wasn't getting his way so he was going to resort to idle threats that he had no intention of acting upon.

"I don't remember my name. Can't remember the last time I ate or even took a shower, for that matter." I tapped my temple. "I hear voices all the time. I used to recognize them and now I don't know who they are. Do you seriously think the sweet promise of death will terrify me? Lose your marbles for a day and then come talk to me."

Something close to pity crossed his face. He sighed before saying, "Your demon can come."

"Oh joy," the panther said.

"He will be on a tight leash, though. One wrong move, and I will kill him."

The demon growled. "It'll take a lot more than a weak-ass fairy to kill me."

I stepped in between the irate-looking fae and the panther. "Okay, I'm ready."

With one last glare for the panther, the fae opened the door and steered me out into the hall toward the stairs. The panther was on my heels.

"Where are we going?" I asked.

"We're leaving," he said, then he smiled down at me. "Out the back, though."

"Good call."

As we descended the stairs, he started to take his hand from me. "Since you seem to be struggling a bit—"

I slammed his hand back down on my arm. "Not when you touch me."

He stopped on the steps and gave me his full attention. "I beg your pardon?"

With my free hand, I tapped a finger to my temple. "So many voices. Your touch quiets them."

"Okay," he said, but I wasn't sure if it was to himself or the crazy girl he was helping down the stairs. "So, since you're struggling, and my touch seems to make you more…"

"Sane? Lucid? Relaxed?"

He wet his lips and avoided eye contact. Poor guy.

"I'm sorry," he said as if he genuinely felt bad for me.

"Why? I could be a serial killer. I mean, if the hotel room upstairs is any validation, then there's actually a pretty good chance that I am."

His eyes swept my body. "I highly doubt that. Usually, women who look like you, who wear cutesy shirts, aren't serial killers."

I actually couldn't remember what I looked like, so I didn't know what he meant by women who looked like me. I'd have to put a pin in it. "Remind me later to revisit this conversation and then act accordingly based on my emotions."

He squinted at me but didn't say a word. His eyes tracked the cat behind me. "Fae might not be able to recognize when a demon lies, but you owe me for taking you to my realm. I expect you to answer truthfully. Do you remember what happened to the demons?"

The panther said, "Don't look at me. I don't remember a thing."

"Oh, you have memory loss, too?" I asked over my shoulder.

The cat pressed into me. "No, sweet face. Someone gave me Don Julio in my kitty bowl."

I winced. I had a feeling it was me. "You know I don't normally go with strange men. Or at least I don't think I do."

The panther reassured me. "If he looks at you the wrong way, I'll eat him."

The fae stopped walking and magic filled the stairway. I watched as a bolt of dust hit the panther, turning him into a small black cat.

"What did he do?" screeched the panther.

The fae kept walking with me in tow. "We can't step outside with a panther. People will have questions."

"*I* have questions," I said as I leaned down and snatched the kitty into my arms. He was cursing in Latin, so I talked louder. "How did five red demons go unnoticed?"

The fae swung us around the last set of steps. "Good question. Once you are more…sane, maybe you can answer that for me."

His head was on a swivel as we exited the hotel.

"Where are these shifters?"

I pointed to an old Buick in front of the hotel. "Those three beefy guys right there."

He stared at them for a bit. Finally, the driver noticed us. He slapped the passenger in the chest before pointing at us. The fae gave them the bird before he pulled me in tight, squishing the kitty between us, and then we disappeared.

As a psychic, I didn't know why I didn't see that coming.

CHAPTER 5

THE FAE RELEASED ME AND THE PURRING KITTY IN A FOREST FILLED with the most beautiful flowers I'd ever seen. Birds sang a sweet tune, and there was such peace surrounding us. I set the kitty down, and he strolled over to a stunning flower that was begging to be touched. The fae grabbed the kitty by the neck at the same time the flower petals opened up, showing gigantic teeth. The flower's mouth chomped down, barely missing the kitty.

The fae growled as he none too gently sat the cat down on the other side of him. "Just because something doesn't look dangerous doesn't mean that it isn't. Don't touch anything in the forest."

The cat gave me an incredulous look. "Really? You didn't see that coming?"

"Whoops," I said.

"Unbelievable," the cat said. He ran his body through the fae's legs. "Pick me up, big fellow."

"I loathe demons," the fae snarled as he tried to kick my cat. "I should have let the plant eat you."

"But you didn't. It could be because you're equally enamored with the pent-up doll over there as I am, or it could be that you're less of a dog man and more of a cat man."

The fae stopped walking. "Neither."

The cat nodded. "Is it because she hasn't showered? I can

promise she has potential underneath that seven-inch layer of dirt."

Aww!

Wait, was that an insult? I lifted an arm and smelled my pit. Gross. Nope, the demon was just telling the truth.

The fae sighed heavily. "The reason I stopped outside of the court is because I don't want anyone to know of our arrival just yet. All fae can create portals to the fae realm if they have royal blood. However, when you create a portal inside the court, everyone is alerted and sometimes it is considered a threat. With my grandfather away, I'm not sure how well I'll be received. So, we will walk to the gates of the summer court and give them plenty of time to understand that I come in peace."

He placed his hand on my back to steer me through the forest, and I immediately sighed. He noticed and gave me another pitying look. As long as he kept his huge hand on my back and the voices stopped, I couldn't care less how he looked at me. "I've been looking for an object that is an important key. I lost it a very long time ago and I have been searching for it ever since. I need to get it back in order to redeem myself."

"You really think Nuts can help you with that?" the cat asked.

The prince nodded. "With proper training she can. You'll have to listen to my every command, though. The both of you."

"I'll do what my master tells me to do," the cat said with a growl.

The fae replied, "You'll do what I tell you to do."

"Sorry, pretty boy, but no. Jo is the only one that can command me."

Call me confused. "I'm your master?"

"Yep," the cat purred. "The way you broke up that witch's coven and freed me was epic. I guarantee they are somewhere planning their revenge as we speak."

The fae stopped walking. His head slowly turned toward me. "Do you know what the demon speaks of?"

I sighed. "No, but it sounds like I'm pretty badass."

He pushed my back to get me walking again. "As soon as we're safe, we'll work on seeing what visions of the future you can call upon."

"As long as you keep a hand on me at all times, I'm willing to do whatever."

The demon snorted. "Man, I wish I had hands. Damn these paws."

"I'm sure that I will have to stand before the royal court and give a testimony as to where I've been and what I've been doing. Once you are clean and presentable, then I'll make the introductions to the court. My grandfather being away on vacation with a friend could be problematic. Hopefully enough time has passed that my uncles and aunts won't be cross with me anymore."

"How long were you gone?" I asked as I sidled closer to him to avoid a plant that was clearly moving my way.

"I have been missing for centuries. I was trapped in a different plane by an evil queen. Honestly, it felt like a month, but time acted differently there."

Mildly intrigued, I said, "So will this be the first time back home?"

He nodded. "Things should be interesting, considering that my grandfather recently abdicated the throne, and my uncle has been ruling since I have been missing."

"Oooh family drama, huh?" the cat asked. "And here I thought the pretty boy was completely boring."

"So," I said, "you're supposed to be king instead of a prince?"

"Yes. My uncle isn't fit to rule."

Something in the back of my mind was struggling to come forward. Did I know a fae prince?

"You sound bitter," the cat said.

"I care nothing for the crown, demon. I do care about the key, though."

"The key you've been looking for?" I asked.

He shook his head. "It will redeem me, and it will free me."

I wasn't at my best, and it had been a while since I had operated on all four cylinders, so instead of asking questions that I was ninety-nine percent sure I would forget I just said, "Awesome."

"Wait," the cat said, "you're a prince?"

The fae nodded.

The cat started mumbling something in Latin. Then the cat looked up at me. "Um...dollface, we need to talk. In private."

The fae dropped his arms by his sides and started to argue with the cat but I ignored them both as a vision came to me. I instinctively knew that the vision I was receiving was from the past. Maybe it was because my body felt like it was being rewound. My eyes lost focus as an elderly woman whom I semi-recognized tilted her head back and laughed a beautiful sound. She said, "I do like you, Jolene. A lot. I can't wait until that fae prince stumbles upon you. You will show him who's boss." Blood dripped from my nose as the vision faded into another. "I've already told you that you will go up against the fae prince. Whether you will be the victor or not is totally up to you."

"She's bleeding again," the cat said.

The prince put his hand on my arm. "Oh, jeez, sorry."

The vision left me, and the beautiful forest came back into view. I pulled up the bottom of my shirt and gently pushed it against my nose to staunch the flow of blood. My legs felt like rubber, and my chest was having a hard time expanding enough to get me the oxygen that my lungs needed. I had to act like I had my stuff together, though. If that vision showed me anything it was that the man walking beside me could be my enemy.

"Um...I really need to have a powwow with you, Nuts."

"Not now," the fae prince said.

My head was spinning, and honestly, I wanted a nap more than a conversation. The fae prince started ushering me through the forest.

The gardens slowly faded away to ashes and ruins. The fae prince's blond brows drew together as we continued to walk up a road of dirt and debris. The stench in the air was enough to make me gag.

"I don't understand," the prince said. "Our kingdom is made up of four courts, their locations arranged into an S-shape. The spring court is below us. I placed us in the forest before the summer court." He stopped in his tracks and put his hands on his narrow hips. "Above us to the left are rolling hills that make up the fall court, and a few days' ride beyond that is the winter court." He pointed to snow-topped mountains that seemed so far away. "See, that is the winter court. I've never seen this area before."

The cat whistled. "Wow, you have been away for a long time. From what I've heard, your world has changed a lot. You didn't even mention No Man's Land."

The fae prince said, "What?" at the same time I asked, "What's No Man's Land?"

"It is fae that belongs to none of the four courts, lesser fae, and fae that have been exiled from their kingdoms for various reasons," the cat said. "Basically, it's the slums. We're crazy for walking through here."

A vision came as fast as it went, because luckily the prince put his hand on the small of my back. All I had seen was that we would never make it to the summer court. I didn't know where we would end up, but it would be nowhere near where he intended.

Truth was, we probably needed clarity and answers right now, but my head was pounding. I was totally okay with walking in blind to whatever trouble lay ahead of us. At least I wasn't passing out and forgetting the cat's name again. Ugh. Dang it. What was the cat's name?

"The land almost looks scorched," the prince said, his voice filled with horror. "How could this have happened?"

I sighed heavily. I wasn't going to remember this conversation in the morning. I knew that I needed to be here, though. The woman that was in those visions was the same woman who instructed me to come here today. I might not remember her, but my gut was telling me that I had to trust her. I rubbed my temple. She had said something about a connection. A spark. Salvation. I eyed the prince. His touch did quiet the voices. Was he…my mate? How could I forget! She said that a fae prince was my mate. I was staring at the fae prince as he was turning in circles, looking lost.

The cat slunk over to me. "Never mind the talk. I am sensing that you just figured out who that could be?"

I nodded and then frowned.

"I know, dollface. It's a bit disappointing."

The fae prince was cute. He seemed to be nice. I could do

worse, but there was something that just wasn't connecting for me. I squatted down to pet the cat, and he purred.

"I shouldn't be disappointed. Isn't finding your mate a rare thing?"

"Yeah," the cat said, "but it's okay to be disappointed. Honestly, fate screwed you on this one. I say you give that biatch the finger. He's too…too…it's like he's a cross between preppy and Hollywood."

I knew what he was insinuating, but the cat obviously thought he was doing a bad job of conveying his thoughts. He continued. "I mean, you're the villain of my favorite fairytale, and he's not…"

"Badass enough?"

"Yep," the cat answered. "He's soft. Like a Ken doll."

I scratched him under his chin, making him purr louder. "Question, if I'm not the villain you think I am, are you still going to love me?"

"I've already eliminated the possibility that you don't eat small children. But I've also already witnessed that you don't cry over spilled blood."

I watched the fae prince mumbling something under his breath while he threw his arms up. Turning my attention back to the cat, I asked, "Meaning?"

"Those demons in the hotel room, well you killed them. It was the hottest thing I've ever seen in my life, and I have lived a long time."

My eyes widened. "Me?" He nodded. "But you told the fae that you couldn't remember."

"Yeah, I lied. It happens. A lot, actually. But not to you, dollface." His gaze darted over to the fae. "I just don't think everyone should know how badass you are. Not until we are sure that you can rely on your powers without them glitching."

"How badass are we talking?"

"I mean, I've seen some things but—"

"This is unbelievable," the fae prince interrupted as he walked over to us with a frown. "I don't know what is going on. One thing is for certain, we don't need to dally here. Let's continue before it gets dark."

I wanted to have a private conversation with my cat, but

instead I found myself being ushered down the rough terrain. As soon as we reached the bottom of the small hill, we saw another fae. There was no doubt that these people were on the brink of starvation. Most had tattered clothes that showcased their protruding ribs. I swallowed heavily as the cat jumped up in my arms and swiveled his head, trying to look everywhere at once.

None of the people really stopped to look at the strangers as we passed them on the road. They were too busy trying to get to wherever they called home before the night ended.

"Fear," the cat said. "I can smell it on all of them."

"Yes," I replied, "but what are they afraid of? That's the question."

We passed by a tiny little boy who ran across the road to what looked like a bar. He pulled the huge, heavy door open and then yelled, "The assassins are coming!" Then he turned and ran down the broken sidewalk.

"Should we be afraid?" I asked the prince.

He cleared his throat. "I'm not sure. I don't know of these assassins he speaks of."

He gave me a smile as if to try to calm my nerves, and the demon murmured under his breath something about weak-ass princes. He dropped onto all fours as he patrolled ahead. I might be on the fence about the prince, but I freaking adored the cat.

We continued marching along the path as it went from lush grounds to something more apocalyptic. The flowers had lost their color, and even though there was a strength to them, they looked ominous. The wind blew ashes across the dry dirt, and I silently wondered if the prince's court was still standing. I dodged every flower or vine that snaked my way as we continued our trek in silence. If the assassins were anything like their forest, we would be in for a treat.

CHAPTER 6

THE CAT WHINED WITH ANXIETY AS THE UNEVEN ROAD WIDENED and became busier. Someone rammed into my shoulder as they passed me, only to snarl at me as if it were my fault. The cat hissed in response, and I tightened my hold on the ball of fur to make sure he didn't pounce on the sickly-looking fae. We had followed the prince between two food carts when we heard shouts along with the sound of hooves in the distance. It was clear that some people were happy to hear the sound while others recoiled in fear. Who were the men on the horses?

The cat's tail was flicking back and forth. "I don't like this, Nuts. Not one bit. The prince seems lost."

I agreed.

The cat whispered. "I mean, did you hear any voices that told you to come here?"

I nodded and the cat seemed to be digesting that.

"The good news is I haven't seen our deaths." I looked down into his yellow eyes. "Should I just call you 'cat'?"

"You've asked me this question before, dollface."

There was a little girl standing on the side of the road under a sign that read "Fae Spirits." Her dress was clean, but her shoes were soiled, probably from the street filled with garbage and urine. A tired-looking woman grabbed the little girl by the hand and jerked her roughly behind her as two men marched down the sidewalk. One was skinny and tall, the clear opposite of his comrade, who was short and fat. Both wore collars with spikes. I stopped in my tracks and watched as the mom exhaled the moment the men passed.

Not noticing my attention was elsewhere, the cat said, "My name is Fatimah, but you've given me many nicknames. Once you were a little tipsy on Don Julio and we were watching *Scarface*. You were trying your best at a Spanish accent and failing miserably. You shortened my name to Fat. Then you learned the Spanish word for fat, which is *gordo*. For a day I was Gordo."

"Sorry about that," I mumbled as I continued to watch the two large men. They were dressed very nicely considering it looked like we were walking through the slums. Everyone they passed jumped out of their way. They turned a corner and were out of my view.

"It was hilarious," the cat continued. "It was the first time I ever truly remember laughing. Also, I'm not like the fae prince. Soft, you know."

The prince had doubled back to see why it was taking us so long. He said dryly, "If you could please keep up the pace that would be great."

I gave him my best fake smile. "You look as lost as I feel ninety percent of the time. Do you actually have a destination in mind?"

If the prince was offended, he didn't show it. "Of course I do." A frown came across his face. "I just didn't know about this section before the summer court."

I jerked my head toward a fancy woman that was glowering at merchants as she walked by. They jumped from her path as if one accidental touch would have their skin melting from their bodies. "Have you noticed that the people here are terrified of some of the fae?"

He lifted a shoulder. "Perhaps they are high fae."

"Hanging out here?" I looked around at the overcrowded street and dilapidated buildings with the dirty fae scurrying to and fro like scared rats.

"To be honest with you, this…" He made a motion with his hand as if he was trying to encompass everything. "Didn't exist when I lived here." He grabbed my elbow. "We don't have time to worry about the peasants. We have to get to the summer court unless you would like to find dwellings amongst these low class fae."

My eyes narrowed to slits. "Be careful, prince, your assholeness is showing."

The cat howled. "Booyah. Take that, pretty boy. Whew. I felt the burn from here. Is my fur singed?"

The prince growled, and I tightened my hold on Fatimah. None of us spoke anymore as we crossed yet another bridge. This one seemed to be taking us away from the overcrowded town. Towering, muscular men and women dressed in black attire strolled the bridge. Each had a wicked blade in their hand or on their person. Their eyes narrowed in on us as they watched us walk across the bridge. They had the whole intimidating factor down pat. I was truly impressed.

"How far away are we from the sea?" I asked as my boots ground into shells.

"Those aren't shells, love," the cat said as he shook in my arms. "Those are bone fragments."

"Wow," I said as the soldiers watched us as if we were no threat at all. "If we live through this, Fatimah, will you remind me of how epic this all was?"

"I'd call you crazy, but that's like telling an ogre he smells, a vampire that he will crave blood." He eyed me warily. "Or my new friend, Nuts, that she's crazy."

I ran my hand affectionately over his black head. "You're so cute."

"Do you two not see the situation that we are in? Tread carefully," the fae prince snapped.

"Oh, no we see," I said nodding at a fae warrior. She arched a brow at me as if I amused her. They were totally listening in on our conversation. "We are treading carefully on bones. Whose bones? We don't know. It could be their fallen enemies, or it could be their ancestors. Maybe they have a necromancer put the pieces back together every once in a while and let the dead have an immortal game of revenge."

The fae prince stopped walking to look at me. "You are going to get us killed."

I shrugged. "I haven't seen my death so I can't confirm that."

Whatever the prince was saying fell on deaf ears as a vision rushed to me almost too quickly to decipher. I sighed heavily as the vision faded. There was no good way to stop the chain of events. All that I could do was make sure that Fatimah and I were not caught in the middle.

As soon as we were past the watchful eyes of the sentry, three men appeared. They were wearing fancy clothes and had a menacing look on their faces. I had approximately twenty seconds. One of the men slapped the other man in the chest before pointing at us.

The large one with a square face said, "And where do you two think you are going?"

The prince tilted his head up and said, "The summer court. Please get out of our way."

They snickered as they mimicked the prince's haughty voice. Then the short red-haired man said, "You've entered our territory now and there is no passing on to other courts—"

"Even if you could," the large one scoffed.

"Without payment," the short red-haired man finished.

"I'm not paying you! I'm a prince. You will remove your bodies from my presence at once."

The three men took on a whole new gleam in their eye. "Prince, you say? In No Man's Land?" When the tall, skinny one reached for something in his waistband, I held on to the cat while jumping to the right. An iron net shot out of his hand, fully enclosing the prince and making him fall to the crushed-boned path.

The prince shouted obscenities before his eyes jerked to mine. "A warning would have been nice."

Fatimah snickered in my arms until the men's attention turned to me. I stroked the kitty as the sound of hooves pounded down the path. Mounted soldiers clad in black attire came upon the scene.

The white-blond-haired man I assumed was the leader shouted, "What is going on here?"

One of the fae men backed up slowly. He glanced at the other two before he snarled, "We were just having a bit of fun, as is our right."

The presumed leader ticked up his chin. "We will see about that, won't we?"

Another set of hooves made their way toward us, parting the five horses and the soldiers who sat on top. A man who was at least six-foot-three with coal-black hair and eyes the color of wheat slowly dismounted his horse and walked toward us. He was one of those rare males who if you saw casually walking on the street you would stop in your tracks and try to be discreet while simultaneously making sure that you weren't drooling. I closed my mouth just to be on the safe side.

His hypnotic eyes were staring at the prince, who was a little tied up at the moment, so I let my eyes travel over him. His jaw was clenched, and his nose was flaring with each long inhale that he took. He had on a black T-shirt that molded to his body in such a perfect way, I wondered if it had been sewed onto him. Black ink curled underneath the sleeves and ran down his forearm. Dear heavens, even his forearms were sexy. I wasn't sure if I was into bad boys, but with the way my belly was tightening, I was leaning toward *most definitely*. This man was thirty percent captivating and seventy percent intimidating, and I was one hundred percent here for it.

The cat was purring in my arms. "I have never before questioned my sexuality so hard."

The man's eyes jerked to Fatimah and then they landed on me. He was definitely intimidating, but I was crazy, so I held his stare. He stopped when he was three feet in front of me.

Totally ignoring the incapacitated fae, he barked at me, "Who are you?"

"Um..."

"Nuts," Fatimah whispered.

I nodded. "Yeah, now it's coming back to me. I'm crazy. You don't have to tell me your name, I'll just forget anyways."

He continued to stare at me. None of the people behind him moved. I wasn't sure if they were even breathing.

Finally, the man said, "So you are the one who would dare bring a traitor and a demon into my domain?"

"Well, I mean, I guess so. I am standing here holding the demon." My brows came together. "Or did you mean that as a rhetorical question?"

One of the soldiers gasped.

Fatimah curled in a tighter ball. "I have a bad feeling about this. Maybe you should stop listening to the voices in your head."

"Silence!" the man in front of me commanded. His gaze turned to the fae caught in the net. "Calhoun, it's been a while."

"It has."

"Why are you darkening the fae realm?"

Calhoun hitched up his chin. "I have been in a cursed land. Finally, being free, I decided to come home. We are on our way to the summer court. Some things have obviously changed while I've been gone."

"Why did you not portal there?" the dreamy guy asked.

When the fae prince didn't answer, I raised my hand, causing the intimidating guy to swing his gaze my way. "I think I can actually answer this one." He arched his brow. "The prince wanted to give the summer court time to prepare for his arrival."

The man in front of me snorted. "Sure he did. More like he's weak and he didn't think he could get through the summer court's wards."

The fae prince growled underneath the net. "I've come back home to regroup before finding the key."

A sneer crossed the man's face, but instead of detracting from his beauty, it made him even sexier. "The one you lost over a woman."

"Should you be jealous?" Fatimah whispered to me.

I looked down at the cat. "I'm not sure. Should I be?"

The cat let out a sound that was eerily close to a groan. "What are the voices saying, Nuts?"

"I don't know. They're quiet. I'm only getting glimpses from the past. Like fuzzy reminders." Something dawned on me as a horrific image floated across my brain. "I hope these people don't have a chainsaw."

"Literally, it was a movie," the cat hissed. "You've got to move on from this or else it'll be only cartoons in our future. I can stomach a lot but not that. Not even for you, sugar tits."

I could feel the beefcake's gaze on me. When I made eye contact with him, it took everything I had not to take a step back from his intense stare.

His gaze swung to the three fae who were clearly the problem here. My eyes went to the collars the men were wearing as the prince said, "And what are you three doing here?"

The short one must've been the appointed spokesman. "We have the day off from the court, but that doesn't matter. We don't answer to you."

The blond male cleared his throat. "Sir, these are the three that I had reports on earlier. The ones that killed the shopkeeper and his family."

The smexy man nodded with a smile. "Ah, I've been looking for you three." Then he clapped the man on the back, and I watched in semi-horror as his hand heated. Less than a second is all it took to take the man's flesh from his bones. I literally blinked and the flesh was gone. Melted. The skeletal remains crumbled to the bridge. At least now we knew how the bone fragments came to be.

Fatimah whispered. "And that's a real villain."

The two fae men with the collars tried to make a run for it, but they didn't get very far. The two soldiers struck them down with their blades.

The fae prince was still under the net. He cleared his throat. "Now that that has been dealt with, please remove me from this iron net."

The hot villain looked at me instead of the fae prince. He didn't break eye contact.

"Erm…I know that we're not going to make it to the summer court, but I feel like I should do my due diligence and ask anyway: Can you let us pass?"

"I don't know what kind of joke this is, but I don't have time for it." He looked over his shoulder. "Cadence, take them to the dungeon."

"Wait!" the fae prince said. "You can't hold me hostage, I'm a prince!"

I shook my head as I said to Fatimah, "Ooh, the entitlement with this one."

"A prince that is in *my* domain," the hot villain announced. "A prince whose people have turned their back on. A prince that has brought a…" He looked at me with a sneer. "A non-fae and a demon into our world."

I rolled my eyes. "A whole lot of prejudice is being thrown our way. I bet this place has horrible reviews."

The fae prince started shouting, but I heard none of his words as a vision came to me. Flashes of images were pushed at me. I needed the vision to stop, but it wouldn't. The world became dizzy, and my knees hit the hard, crushed bones. I barely remember Fatimah jumping from my arms as the blood dripped between my palms.

Two strong hands jerked me to my feet and the vision quieted. I stared up at the man who had a murderous look on his face. I felt like I was either going to pass out or throw up, but first I had a message to deliver.

"Your tip was wrong. Your friend Shay isn't going to track down a ruthless killer." My head went to my throat because the man in the vision wore a collar. "He has been ambushed. They are torturing him. They want to know why he was searching for one of theirs. Who is behind the hunt? How long has it been going on? How strong are your numbers?" Shay's agony rippled through the vision, and I squeezed my eyes so tightly that I saw stars. Breathless, I continued, "He is in the warehouse. Hidden room. Blue and white walls lead to the staircase." My legs were trembling. "He won't make it another day. You have to go now. Wait for the wolf to howl and then scale the wall."

I was waiting for him to call me crazy or toss me on the floor. I mean it wouldn't be anything that I hadn't heard before. Memory or not, I was certain.

His beautiful eyes raked over my face. "Cadence, take the fae prince and the demon to a cell. If I don't make it back by morning light with Shay, I want you to kill the prince slowly. Make sure he sees every organ pulled from his body before his last breath is taken. Skewer the demon on a pike beside the prince."

My eyes shot up. Now that was good imagery. Like standing ovations and a round of applause.

A woman's voice came from somewhere behind the pillar of a man holding me up. "This could be a trap."

"It could be," he answered.

When he didn't add more, the woman sighed. "If you don't return, every court will hear his screams, my lord. Then I will find her and make her wish she never graced our realm."

"Mattia, prepare our elite force. Have all twelve of them meet me on the bridge."

I shook my head. "It will be just four, due to the scouts who are waiting for you. Horses and no portals. When you create portals, everyone within a mile radius can feel the power. Stealth is your friend." My nose was dripping blood again. "And fog. You will wait for the wolf's howl, and then you will take the magic down where the hawks' talons fight one another."

After my last word, I passed out, not caring if the so-called lord took my advice or not.

CHAPTER 7

I woke up on a horse, and my bones were being jostled. Where was I? The cat! I had a cat. His name was Fatty. I moved in the steel arms that were holding me firmly against a solid chest. My head was cradled in a well sculpted arm that was giving me a crick in my neck. I peered up at the hot male and gave myself a mental high-five for recognizing him. Maybe even crazy could recognize hot.

"You're awake. Good. I need to let you know that if you have led me astray, I will gut you slowly, letting your intestines trail behind you as I drag your body through the streets."

"Man, you are awesome at this. You should so get some quotes made on some T-shirts. Open up a little store with some witty crop tops advertised in the shop window. You'd make a killing. Pun intended."

"You jest, but I can assure you that I'm deadly serious."

I yawned. "Cool. If you don't want business advice, just say so." I shifted again and groaned. "This is a really uncomfortable position. Would you mind if I sat up?"

With one hand he halfway flung me into a sitting position without ever slowing down his horse.

"Where's my cat?" I asked.

"Your demon, you mean? He is in a cell as well."

"That's super cruel...but I would expect no less from a man with such fantastic visual one-liners."

"You talk too much."

Maybe. I couldn't remember. Usually I recalled hardly anything after I slept, and yet I remembered this man, the cat, the fae prince and where we were headed. Maybe this realm was healing me.

"Now you have nothing to say," he said.

I watched the branches, making sure the beast I was on wouldn't accidentally run me under a low hanging one. "I wouldn't know if I talk too much. I'm crazy as a bat. My memories have faded."

I felt his chest take a deep breath in before releasing the air. "You think you are truly a psychic?"

I squeezed his thigh as the horse jumped over a fallen log. "Visions, voices, bloody nose, all signs of being psychic? Then yes that's what I'm claiming."

"If it's true then it sounds as if you don't know how to embrace your gift. It also sounds like you're losing your mind."

"Oh, that reminds me, don't hurt..." What was his name? Caden? Carson? "The pretty boy I came with. I'm pretty sure he's my ticket to the voices stopping." And possibly my mate.

"The voices won't stop until you're dead."

I laid the back of my head against his chest. I didn't care if he didn't like my rat's nest hair tickling his chin. I was tired. "Something to look forward to then."

The horse started to slow. "I need you to be very quiet now. If you speak, I will cut out your tongue."

It wasn't as poetic, but I got the point. I nodded.

He jumped from the horse and then none too gently grabbed me by the waist and hauled me off. Once my boots touched the ground, he handed his horse off to one of the two men he had brought. He leaned down to my ear and whispered, "I will shroud us in the fog. No one will see us if we don't make a noise. I will carry you to make sure you don't alert them with your heavy footsteps. Do not speak."

I gave him the thumbs up. He picked me up and threw me over one shoulder like a sack of wheat. Then we waited and waited. I propped my chin in my hands, unintentionally digging my elbows into his back. It was very muscular. He probably didn't feel a thing and therefore I had no guilt.

In the distance a wolf howled, and a grin lit my face. The man was carrying me along when the two others started to maneuver their way out of the forest. He came within twelve feet of the building and stopped right under a sign of two hawks engaged in a battle. The sign read, "Hawk Brothers Feed and Supply Store." He stood me on my feet while he placed his hands in the air. His eyes closed and magic pulsed from him. The moment the ward dropped, the wind rustled and I wanted to clap, but I really didn't want to lose my intestines.

He snagged me with one arm and chucked me none too gently back over his massive shoulder. I wiggled a little, and a warm hand clamped my bottom and squeezed. I tried not to move as the man carrying me took out a dagger and stuck into the stone wall of a medium sized castle. Two blades popped out from the boots he was wearing and though the sound of the blades coming out was minimal, it made him freeze for a few precious seconds. Then he began to scale the wall with me precariously balancing on his shoulder. I couldn't wait to tell the cat about this so that he could remind me if I forgot. This was hands down the coolest thing I had ever witnessed. Or at least I thought it was. Maybe I saw assassins working all the time and this was just another day of badassery for me?

At the top of the wall, the other two assassins leaned over and plucked me from the shoulder of the man who had carried me. They halfway flipped me in unison, so I landed on my feet.

One of the men whispered. "There are four on the roof, my lord."

I shook my head and held up five fingers.

"Watch her," he said.

They bowed their heads, and then Hotness wrapped himself in fog and disappeared like a shadow through the night. Seconds later he reappeared. His stony gaze landed on the male to my right.

"I disabled them. There were five."

"I'm sorry, my lord." He nervously shuffled his feet. "I only saw four."

I raised my hand, and three sets of eyes swiveled my way. "Yes?" the lord asked.

"The fifth one was coming up the stairs to the roof. Your friend here literally didn't see him."

"But he should have heard him," the lord said. "And I don't believe I asked you."

I crossed my arms over my chest. "Be careful. I'm crazy. You can't predict crazy."

"Not another word," he said as he grabbed my hand and pulled me in the direction of the stairs. Hugging the wall, they were practically silent as they descended the steps. In fact, I was the only loud one. Tall, dark, and handsome was aware of my limited stealth mode if his clenched jaw was any indication. I rolled my eyes. Then I jerked my hand out of his and took my boots off. Holding them with one hand, I walked down the next few steps in my socks. I wiggled my way through the two men in front of me. One reached out to snag my elbow, but the lord waved him off. At the end of the steps, I took a left, and without looking both ways, I quietly went down the hall. I had already seen this. We had thirty seconds before the last door on the right opened. I picked up the pace and waved to the guys hurriedly. Quickly I opened the third door on the left. I waved them on. You couldn't really see their bodies, but there was a thick fog moving over the carpet at a rapid pace. I held the door open wider, and when the last of the fog literally rolled in, I shut the door, holding one finger over my mouth.

The second the door clicked shut, we all heard a door further down opening, and then multiple footsteps passed our room as the fae continued down the hall. Once it was clear, I turned to face them. Cutting through the fog and accidentally stepping on someone's foot, I made a beeline for the bookshelf behind the only desk in the room. My hand ran down the right side of the wood casing. Once I found the hidden button, I pressed it, opening a secret door to the right of the bookcase. Without waiting to see if the boys were following, I crept down the narrow staircase. Once I got halfway, I paused. The guy with the short, curly blond hair became visible as he stopped next to me. Once my eyes adjusted to the darkness, I pointed down the stairwell and held up two fingers.

Mr. Hotness shouldered past us and then ten seconds later he came up the stairs and waved us on. At the bottom of the landing, I stepped over one of the fallen fae and then squatted down to take the keys attached to his belt. Standing, I jerked my thumb to the right. With one hand on my back, the leader pushed me along until I dug in my heels and pointed to the right. With the pair of keys I handed him, he opened a metal door. I wanted to tell him that only two fae, the one that put the ward in place and the one in the cell, could cross the magic barrier, but I really liked my tongue in my mouth. I silently stood to the side and waited for him to test the barrier. Frustration colored his perfect features when he realized the magic was keeping him out. It would take him too long to take down the barrier. It was time that we didn't have, and he knew it.

I waited impatiently for him to figure out that I wasn't fae. When eyes the color of taffy darted my way, I made the shooing motion with my hand. He stepped back and I waltzed right into the room. A form was slumped in the corner. I knelt beside him and gently shook his shoulder. He was on the edge of death. His body was so damaged from the torment that he was dancing with darkness and no longer cared.

"Hey, buddy," I whispered. "I only have a minute to get you out of this cell so they can start to heal you. Anything longer than that and we won't be on schedule. Can you help me get you to the door?"

The man's eyes flickered open. One hand reached out to cup my cheek. His eyes glistened with unshed tears.

His hand flopped back down to his chest.

"What's your name?"

"Shay," was half groaned out from his parted lips.

"Okay, Shay, I'm going to start dragging you to get you over this magic line. If there is any way you can use your feet to help me, that would be greatly appreciated."

From what I could tell, I had zero muscle and no fat on my

body. I was scrawny. There was no way I could drag Shay by myself. Luckily, I knew that he was going to help me.

Together we finally had his right arm over the line. The leader grabbed Shay's forearm and had him out in the hallway with one pull.

One of the men said, "I'll carry him. We can heal him when we get him to the horses."

Surprisingly, the leader looked at me with a question in his eyes.

I shook my head and whispered. "Heal him now or say your goodbyes."

The man with the tight blond curls argued. "It'll take our lord at least five minutes to get Shay to the point he can stand."

My eyes met the leaders. "If you hurry, you'll have twenty seconds to spare."

Without another word, the leader put his gigantic palm on top of Shay's chest. I could feel the magic in the air. Another vision was coming to me. Huh. Didn't see that one coming. I squatted low just in case this one was a doozy. I didn't want to hit the pavement. I wasn't certain that they wouldn't leave me here.

Strong hands gripped my waist and pulled me near. My back hit the chest of a male. My soul was content. My mind was...not broken. There was a connection there. A bond. Just like the old woman had said. The man was my salvation. My ticket off the crazy train.

The vision faded before I could see either of our faces.

When my eyes came back into focus, the leader made eye contact with me. One brow rose.

I shook my head. "Nothing you need to know."

After a few more minutes, Shay was able to sit up with help and he had a little bit of color back in his face.

The leader stood up. "You two carry him. I'll make you a path."

I held up both my hands, making the time out gesture. "Or we could go back the exact same way we came and we won't run into a soul. By the time they find the first fallen fae we will have a ten-minute advantage. They won't catch up with us." I added, "We shouldn't fight today."

He weighed my words and then nodded. Quickly we retraced

our steps, and the assassins had no issue with me leading the way. When I paused, they paused. If time wasn't of the essence, I would've totally messed with them. After they had thrown Shay over a horse and everyone was ready to go, I snapped my fingers.

"Dang it."

"What is it?" he asked.

I pointed to my socks. "I forgot my boots. I don't remember where I set them down." I shifted a little, even though there was no room. I wanted to see his face. His eyes locked onto mine, but his face registered no emotion.

"It will be fine. If they use a locator spell to find you, I'll meet them at the door."

So hot. I yawned then snuggled back into his arms. "I wasn't worried about them finding me. I was worried about my boots. They were super cool. Oh well. Probably won't remember that I ever had a pair tomorrow."

He turned the horse and, at a breakneck pace, started back the way we came, which looked like it was on the outskirts of town. I was so tired, but I fought sleep. I really wanted to remember today for as long as I could. I was certain that there were pieces of today that would hopefully change my future for the better.

CHAPTER 8

No one spoke when we crossed the bone-covered bridge and took a trail up a hill. The area was still rough looking, but nothing compared to the village that we had entered when we first arrived. There wasn't a stench of urine, and the passing people didn't look as terrified.

"How many villages are here?"

I thought he wouldn't answer, but finally he said, "Too many."

There was a large, black building that looked as if it had been thrown together with magic. Could anyone actually build something that beautiful without the use of magic? There was a small cabin to the right. Instead of passing it, our small group came to a stop. The leader helped me down from the horse and instructed his two men to take Shay to the infirmary. He grabbed my elbow and ushered me into a small cabin that was at least half a mile away from the main castle.

Once inside he said, "I should put you in a cell with your friend." He shook his head. "I'm not entirely sure that you weren't sent here to destroy everything that I've built."

"That's fair."

His lips twitched. "Are you not going to ask me what I've built?"

I cocked my head to the side. "Not sure that I care."

"That's fair," he repeated my words back to me. "There is a

bathroom to the left. As soon as you get in the shower, I'll have some clothes put by the sink for you and food brought in. When's the last time you ate?"

I shrugged, and his eyes narrowed on my slim frame.

"I'll get you food while you shower. After you have eaten you will answer my questions."

I yawned again but made my way to the shower. Over my shoulder I said, "I'll tell you what, big guy, I'll answer what I remember." I laughed at that. "Oh, and I want my cat! Bet you thought I'd forget about him." At the door, I turned to look at him. He wore a look somewhere between confused and enraged. "Honestly, I thought I would too, so don't be all upset." Before he could say anything, I went into the bathroom and shut the door behind me.

I would take a quick shower, eat, and answer as many obnoxious questions as that leader would fling my way. If I hurried then I could get to sleep sooner and hopefully recharge a little.

At least that was the plan. But as soon as the warm water hit me, there was no hurrying. I was in heaven, and did people hurry in heaven? No. There was no such thing as the restraints of time. I washed my hair three times. That's how many times it took to get the dirt out of it. I scrubbed every inch of my body until it was red. The scent was a musky, woodsy smell that I recognized from the leader. I'm not going to lie; the smell was divine. This must be his home. It was a pity I wouldn't remember that handsome face tomorrow. Then again, I had dozed off a few times since being in this realm and had still remembered things. It must be the fae magic. I wondered if they would allow me to live here…

When I got out of the shower, there was a pile of men's clothes lying next to the sink. I had been enjoying my shower so much I hadn't even heard the door open. The sweatpants had a drawstring that I pulled as far as it would allow, and then I rolled the bottom of the pants. The T-shirt hung to my knees. With no bra, I decided to put on the heavy sweatshirt too. I looked like a vagrant, but I was clean and warm and that's all that really mattered.

I padded barefoot out of the bathroom and found the leader

waiting for me in front of a fire. My demon cat was on the hearth, flicking his tail. The leader's gaze traveled down the length of my body, no doubt taking in my questionable appearance. When his eyes drifted back to mine, there was a good amount of appreciation written all over his face.

My cat was back and he was lounging on a stool close to the kitchen. He purred. "Wow. You were gorgeous with the dirt but now you are like…better than catnip."

The leader never took his eyes from me as he said to the demon, "You're not really a cat."

"I'm not really a man either, but Nuts is over there making me wish all kinds of things."

The leader cleared his throat and made his way over to a long couch. With a wave of his hand, he silently offered me a place to sit.

I sat down on the white couch and curled my feet underneath me. "Hey, Fat…"

"Fatimah," the cat replied as he jumped down from the stool and came closer to me. "Don't worry. I'll remind you again tomorrow."

I gave him a bright smile.

The leader said, "I'm Evander, and you are?"

I looked at the cat and he sighed. "She doesn't remember."

He crossed his arms over his chest. "Can you at least tell me why you are here?"

"The voices told me to come," I said, like he was the one that was slow on the uptake.

"Who are these voices?"

Fatimah stopped licking himself. "Do you think she honestly knows? I mean, at first I just thought she was a crazy chick because, believe it or not, I'm kind of a magnet for them." Fatimah turned to me. "But I was wrong. Well, I mean, she could still be crazy, but my point is she sees things, man. Past, present, and future. And there are a whole bunch of people in all those timeframes just yapping at her nonstop."

Evander looked over at the cat. "Demon, can you feel my power?"

The cat jumped down from the hearth and walked in a circle

before lying down on the rug in front of the fire. "Yes. It's more power than the demon lord that I'm under."

"If either of you lie to me, I'll use that power. Do you understand?"

Fatimah looked at me. "Geesh. Talk about trust issues."

Evander's hypnotic eyes landed on me. I didn't know whether to squirm in my seat or fan myself.

"How well do you know the fae prince?" he asked.

I looked at the cat, then Evander. "I just met him."

"And yet you came with him to my world?"

"I'm here because a voice told me to come. She is very persistent, and sometimes ignoring her isn't an option." As Evander studied me unabashedly, I quickly became lost in my own thoughts. I bit my lip hard enough to draw blood. "I guess I'll just go ahead and put this out there so my cat can remind me tomorrow. I think the prince…what was his name?"

Fatimah answered, "I think Calhoun."

"Yeah, I should probably try to remember that. Anyway, I think he's my mate."

The cat piped up, "It's unfortunately true. I think she had a vision of him, and he's her mate."

The room grew eerily quiet. Then Fatimah started making an awful sound like he was about to throw up a hairball.

Without looking at the cat, Evander said, "Throw up on my rug and I will kill you without moving a muscle."

I nodded. Coolest day ever. The level of badassery that one has to acquire in order to kill something without moving was epic.

Finally, Evander asked, "Why would you think that he's your mate?"

Fatimah answered for me. "The voices told her that the fae prince was her ticket to sanity." He added, "But she makes crazy look good, so I don't think she needs him. All I'm saying is let's weigh all our options before we strike them from the board."

I stuck out my bottom lip in a fake pout. "You don't like my mate? We're going to be a family, so unless you don't want to be in the family portraits, you better fake it."

The cat chuckled. "You see! It's things like that that make me fall deeper in love. Like, I'm pretty sure she's kidding, but there's always that chance that I'm wrong."

Evander was studying me like I was the most fascinating thing he had ever come across. "I'm assuming you don't control your visions?"

"No, they are smashed into my head."

His jaw clenched as if the next words were going to pain him. "I will work with you. It will be a long process, but I believe that together we can reverse the damage that has already been done."

"What's the catch?" Fatimah asked.

Evander looked at the cat coolly. "The Winter King is building an army. His kingdom is magically barred so no one can enter or leave unless the king himself grants them access. I want to know how many soldiers he has in his army." He turned to me. "I want you to get well enough to give me those numbers."

"Or?" I asked.

With no emotion he replied, "I'll kill the demon, then your prince, then you."

"Option one!" Fatimah shouted.

My head swung toward the cat. "What? You don't want to weigh all our options now?"

Evander cleared his throat. "You will be a guest here until I have deemed otherwise."

"*Guest* and *prisoner* must have the same connotation," the cat said as I yawned loudly.

I didn't care if they put shackles on me at this point. There was a possibility that just being here in this realm was my answer for healing.

"How is it that Calhoun is supposed to make you gain back your sanity? Just because he is your so-called mate?" Evander asked. He looked as confuzzled as I usually felt. He didn't bat an eyelash at me being psychic, but telling him my beliefs about the fae prince was really tripping him up.

"Who am I to question fate?"

Fatimah snorted. "That's all you do. Literally nonstop complaining that fate is the daughter of an evil bitch and you don't take orders from her."

I played his words over in my head. "So I'm super funny."

"Most of the time." Fatimah added, "Not when the mate's touch quietens the voices that always want your attention. Then you turn sort of zombie-ish."

A smirk came across Evander's face. "That is telling. Well then, I'm assuming you'll do a lot to protect your mate?"

I didn't like to be threatened, or at least I didn't think that was a part of my personality. "Don't assume too much. I requested the cat to be here and not my mate. Again, I'm crazy. If you don't know how to play with crazy, then keep out of the playground."

"Girl," Fatimah said, "I love the swings. Slides, merry-go-rounds, monkey bars, you name it, I love it. Don't kick me out of the playground. The sandbox is my jam."

"Silence," Evander said. He stood up slowly. My eyes drifted over his fitted pair of black cargo pants and his T-shirt that looked like it would rip if he flexed those gorgeous muscles. When my eyes finally landed on his face, he wore a haughty smile. "Come with me."

I quirked a brow. "To where?"

"My bedroom."

"You know what they say," Fatimah purred, "three is a crowd that everyone wants to be in."

"Excuse me?" I asked. Then I looked at Fatimah. "And just for the record, I'm pretty sure that I'm not into that."

"There is only one room in this cabin. The cat can have the living room, though I'm strongly against allowing a demon to be in my home. I will allow him to stay close to you for now."

"I'm not going with you. I'll sleep out here."

"We're not going to sleep."

I felt myself blushing.

The cat swiped a paw at thin air to get my attention. "Is that a blush? Welp, at least we know that she's not a hoe." He shook his tiny head. "I have never been so disappointed in someone before."

"I'm going to start to heal you," Evander's voice boomed. I had a slight feeling he didn't think the cat was as funny as I did. "I'll need you close to do that, and I'm sure during the process you will eventually fall asleep. The more comfortable you are, the more you will let your guard down. Some of the memories you lost will start to come to you in your dream state. You need uninterrupted sleep in order to heal quicker and regain some of your memories."

I looked at the cat. He was back to licking himself, so I was assuming that he didn't feel that either of us was threatened. I waited for a voice, even the voice of reason, to chime in, but when I didn't hear even the old woman I stood slowly.

As if he could clearly read my uncertainty, Evander said, "I promise you that you will be safe with me. I will not lay a hand on you that could be deemed inappropriate."

I nodded the same time Fatimah said, "Well to be honest with you, Nuts, I wouldn't even go then. I mean, what's the point?"

"I'm close to killing your cat," Evander said in a very monotone voice.

"Hush, Fatty," I said with a wink. "See you in the morning."

The cat jumped onto the couch. "Yeah, I'll give you a crash course on the day's events. I don't know what you would do without me, babe."

I was smiling as I walked into the bare bedroom. There was nothing on the walls. No books or even coffee mugs on the dresser. Only a full bed with a blue quilt, a nightstand, and a lamp.

"Cozy," I said. "So this is your home?"

"You could say that." He took off his shoes and socks. When he went to remove his shirt, I turned to study the absent wall. I heard the sound of a zipper and then a drawer opening. Out of the corner of my eye I caught movement. Evander had changed into a pair of gray sweats. He was lying against the headrest, sans shirt. I studied his tattoo that ran over his left upper pectoral and over his shoulder down his arm. "You coming?" he asked.

Do not laugh. Do not get the giggles. Do not try to be cute or witty right now.

I casually wiped my chin to make sure there was no drool and then I scooted onto the bed. His legs were spread wide. He patted the open area between them. "Come sit here and try to relax."

Try to relax? What sane person could casually crawl between a hot stranger's legs and relax? Oh wait. I was crazy. Crazy could one hundred percent do this. With his steady gaze on me, I crawled over the small bed and knelt before him.

"Turn around and lay against my chest. Close your eyes and try to go to sleep."

I did as he asked. As soon as my back hit his chest, I said, "This is how you'll heal me?"

He laughed at the skepticism in my voice. "I can assure you that I don't have to trick women into my bed." He laid his forearms over my stomach and rested his chin on my head. "I will pour my magic into you. If I consistently work at fixing the cracks, you should start to heal. Trust me."

I yawned again. I had nothing to lose, so why not? The last thing I remember was thinking I would never be able to sleep with someone like Evander holding me bare-chested. Turns out it was the best sleep I could have ever asked for.

CHAPTER 9

The dreams wrapped in memories came that night. Small bits and pieces streamed to me in flashes. Little Reef High School was where I attended with my best friend, Sadie. There were seven keys that could open any of the forty-nine portals that were scattered all over the world. I remembered all the faces I had tried to help along the way. Names of each of the people I now called friends. Each of them had secured a key, one that they would protect with their fated mate. I semi-remembered the story we were told in high school of how each of the Lux had lost their key to the Degenerates. Flashes of the old woman Ariana came to me in bits and pieces. She had been trying to help me.

That morning I woke up feeling rested and had regained a little knowledge of who I was. I was still missing huge pieces and there were giant holes in my memory, but I climbed out of bed with more hope than I'd had in a long time.

Evander was gone from his bedroom. After using the bathroom and splashing water on my face, I decided to wake Fatimah.

He stretched and slowly opened one eye. "Hey, Nuts."

"Hey, Fatty," I replied. "So the assassin healed me a little last night."

"Oh, I bet he did."

I rolled my eyes and snorted. "He did choose his words

unwisely at one point. He said, 'you coming?' and I thought I was going to start giggling like a little girl."

"I would have been purring."

I plopped down on the couch. "So I remembered I have a best friend named Sadie. She has white-blonde hair, green eyes, and a smile that is warm."

He cleared his throat. "Well she sounds cute, hopefully she won't be salty that she's been replaced."

I bit my lip so I wouldn't laugh. "The old lady that I constantly hear, Ariana, she looks like earth. Old, scarred, and has some stories to tell."

"Not going to lie, she sounds scary as hell. I would know since I used to live there."

My eyes went to my bag that was on the floor next to the couch. The black ball that was just thrown inside was the key to portals. If Evander searched my purse, which I was sure he did, he might have skipped right over the object.

"This is going to work out great. I'll be healed in no time." I bit my lip. "There's just one little issue."

"The fae prince, your mate...again, condolences, I'm not a fan. Anywho he is looking for a key so he planned on also using you just like the smexy assassin, but he can't because he's locked up. Is that the one little issue?"

"Um...well that and I can't let anyone know that I have the key."

"Yeah, dollface. Wait! What?"

"I have it."

He blinked his almond-shaped eyes. "Like on you?"

I nodded.

Fatimah stuck his nose in the air. "I know that you had a whole nother life before me, but I don't like to be reminded of it."

I hid my smile. "So anyway, the fae prince needs it to regain his title, but I have this feeling that I'm not supposed to give it to anyone. Not to mention the fact that if we rescue the fae prince and escape, then I won't see Evander anymore, and that means that I won't have anyone to heal me. I need to be healed. What if Calvin or whatever his name is can't heal me like the assassin? Do

I try to help him escape and take the gamble? Or do I stay here and heal, and then try to help him escape?" My voice was rising. "I have friends, Fatimah! I can remember Sadie's name and what she looks like. I have the sweetest Granny ever. I have to regain more memories."

He swiped at me with one of his paws. "It's okay, calm down. Let me think." He did a circle on the couch before sitting once again to face me. "Okay, so we lie. We say we don't know where the key is. You continue to get healed. We help the scary guy find some answers, and when the timing is right, we help the fae prince escape. Then we give him the key once we're behind his kingdom's walls. No harm, no foul."

I cringed a little on the inside. "The fae prince is currently in a cell right now."

"And?"

"I don't know how to do this whole fated-mate thing, but is it kosher to let your significant other rot in a prison cell because you need to be healed?"

The cat's eyes widened a bit. "It's been eight hours. 'Rotting' is a strong word."

I ran my hands through my hair. "I could ask Evander to free us. I could vow to still help him find his answers but convince them we need to get to the summer court. As soon as we're off their land I could help the prince collect his throne but…"

"You might blow the opportunity to get healed."

"What if all fae can heal?" I asked.

"They can't."

"But the fae prince's touch did quieten the voices."

That cat tilted his head to the side. "But does that mean he's helping?"

"The voices hurt."

"Yeah, but if you knew how to control the voices…Here is my suggestion: We don't tell anyone you have the key. Keep getting that gorgeous pound of beef to heal you, and then once you're good, we will spring the fae prince. All's well that ends well."

"I feel like only tyrants say that."

"I've been called worse." Fatimah raised his back leg and began to lick himself. "I love being a cat."

I rolled my eyes. "Where's the assassin?"

"Probably out assassinating people. Melting the flesh off of poor souls."

I chuckled as the front door swung open. There stood the assassin in question. He wore a pair of jeans that hugged his masculine thighs and a fitted army-green T-shirt that made his honey-colored eyes pop even more. One word came to my mind: Breathtaking.

He was eyeing me like he was inspecting every inch. "How do you feel?"

"A little more sane."

He gave me a nod before his eyes swung to the cat. "For the record, I was at a meeting. I haven't assassinated anyone this morning. Not yet."

The cat purred. "So hot."

"I think he was trying to intimidate you," I said to the cat.

"And yet all he did was turn me on."

The assassin growled as he walked into the room. "If the both of you are done trying to infuriate me, I would like for the day to start. I suggest you get up, Psychic, and get dressed. There are some clothes that I had made for you this morning lying on the dresser.

I gave him a salute as I went to change into whatever he had brought. I grabbed the first thing on top a dress and slid it over my head. I ran my hands down the soft, blue-green fabric. There were a pair of ballet slippers on the floor. Putting them on my feet, I shuffled toward the door.

"So what's our plan today, my gladiator beefcake?" Fatimah asked.

The assassin didn't even blink. He just continued to stare at the cat. His gaze swung to me appreciatively, his eyes trailing the fabric. "It fits."

"Perfectly."

Fatimah chimed in. "Yeah, I bet a man like you can take one look at a woman and know her sizing."

"I should have killed him before I began to restore your memory," Evander said. "Then again, there is a ten percent chance that I could end him now and you would forget about it."

I put my hands on my hips. "If you are done threatening my cat, I'd like to know where we're off to."

He went into the kitchen and grabbed a weird-looking fruit. It was shaped like a pear but was pink. "Here, eat this. It'll give you enough energy for the whole day."

I bit into it like I would an apple and moaned at the deliciousness. "This is so good."

Evander swallowed and then cleared his throat. "We will walk through my land, and you will tell me if you get any visions. I'd really like for you to focus on what it is I need to know." He eyed the cat. "Your demon will stay here."

I thought Fatimah would have a problem with that, but he seemed content to curl up on the couch. So much for loyalty. I blinked at my cat, and he stared back. Finally he said, "What?"

"Are you not going to protest to go with me? I mean, what if he tries to melt my flesh from my bones?"

The cat yawned. "He literally just made you clothes. He has no intention of melting anything other than maybe your panties."

Evander looked disgusted with the cat. He shook his head and walked out of the cabin.

I gave a little wave to my pet. "Be back soon."

The moment we were outside and walking in the bright sun, Evander asked, "Did some of your memories return?"

I nodded as I swallowed the bite in my mouth. "Yes. I remember that I have a friend I love, a granny I adore, and I'm not as alone as I once thought I was."

He arched his brow. "Do you remember your name?"

I shook my head. "Not yet."

He lightly grabbed my elbow and steered me the way he wanted me to go. "Are you up for a long walk?"

I nodded.

"I'm going to take you to the other side of the training building," he said.

We started walking along the desolate road at a refreshing pace. Everyone we passed on our stroll looked at me with equal parts wonder and suspicion.

"Ignore them," Evander said. "They are curious about the psychic that freed Shay."

"This place...which court does it belong to?"

"None."

He nodded at a pretty fae woman that passed us on the road. Her dress was tattered at the bottom, but the garment was clean. She gave me a shy smile. As we passed her, she reached into her basket and pulled out a beautiful crown made of pink petals. She tipped her head toward me as she extended it.

"A crown for your lady."

I hesitated to reach out and take it, having no money to pay for it. Evander saw my hesitation, so he gently took the crown from the woman and placed it on my head.

The woman smiled. "She looks like a beautiful queen, my lord."

Without looking at me he said, "Yes, the queen of Doomsday."

The woman's smile faltered, but I laughed.

"Hey," I said, "the crown is heavy, but someone has to wear it."

She looked at us both, fidgeting before giving us a small smile and continuing down the road, her pace a little faster. Maybe my new title made her nervous, or maybe it was the ease with which I accepted it?

I straightened my flowery crown as we walked down the road. We dipped under a tree, and the branches peeled back so they wouldn't touch us.

"Everything is sentient here?" I asked, wondering if the plants were able to perceive or feel things.

He nodded.

"How come the plants and trees aren't attacking us like they did on my trek here?"

"They would never harm me. Not in my own sanctuary."

I ran his words through my mind. "Are you someone special or does the vegetation treat all the assassins with respect?"

"The plants won't hurt any of my people."

"Your people? Yet this isn't a court."

He gave me a dazzling smile. "You are asking a lot of questions."

I took another bite of the fruit. "I'm assuming that this is my first time in your world?"

The fruit rolled out of my hand as a vision came.

Evander, the man beside me, was wrapped in iron chains. His bronze skin blistered under the iron, and his eyes were glazed over from the pain. Someone was taunting him, and a smirk covered his face like he knew something that his captor didn't know. Like he could be freed at any second.

A steady hand stabilized me before I teetered to the ground. As soon as the vision was gone, I looked up into honey-colored eyes.

"Someone is going to capture you. They will put you in a cold dark place. A dungeon, a basement…" I shook my head. "Somewhere damp and there is no light anywhere. They will cover you in iron."

His eyes narrowed before he gave me a jerky nod. Then he put one hand on my back and pushed me toward a small trail. "Let's go sit by the lake."

I stopped walking. "Dude! I just told you someone is going to tie you up like a rotisserie chicken, and you want to go on a stroll?"

He laughed. "I'm not worried."

"Well, from what I saw, you should be."

He grabbed my hand and pulled me toward a bench that was facing the lake. "Worrying about the future isn't in my DNA."

Well, unfortunately it was in mine. I chewed on my lip. I didn't see him dying, but I wasn't entirely certain he was handling this correctly. I would be flipping out.

Power was rippling from him where his hand was on my elbow. He was pushing healing energy into me. He noticed me staring at his hand.

"To give you back your memories it will take more than just a few nights. I worked on healing you for five hours last night and you came away with a friend's name and maybe some other minor details. This will all take time. You have to be patient."

"Are there others that can heal me?"

"Not that I know of." He gave me a smirk as we sat down on the bench. "You'll just have to settle for me."

I heard a loud thud followed by a grunt. My eyes darted across the lake to where two female warriors were fighting with long staffs. Their motions were precise and quick as their muscles flexed under the blows that each of them was delivering. They were beautiful to watch. I looked down at my stick legs and arms with a sigh.

Evander's voice sounded in a soft whisper. "Why do you want to be something or someone that you are not?"

Was it that obvious? I leaned back on the bench. "I'm tired of my powers. My gift. I'm not trying to be a whiny biatch, but I think I drew the short stick." I nodded toward the female assassins. "Sometimes it would be nice to have a redo. Start over."

He was staring at me. I turned to look at him. "What?"

"Nothing." Obviously it was something, but I let it go. "If you want to train like the assassins, I can train you, but you have so much power in your tiny body. If you could learn to control it instead of it controlling you, you would be a force to reckon with."

"This is power?" I snorted. "Getting glimpses of timelines and people trying to wreak havoc or save the world along with pounding headaches and nosebleeds. It feels more like a stone around my neck."

"It's only because you haven't trained for your power."

"And you think the fae realm will help me with that?"

He shook his head. "No, I think *I* can help you with that."

Before I could say anything else, a little boy came running up to Evander to show him a knife that he had made out of wood. I was trying to smile less like a lunatic and more like a friendly visitor as Evander oohed and ahhed over the wooden weapon when a vision came. *The little boy would be playing on the rocks above a waterfall today. He would slip, hit his head, and drown in the water below. He hadn't reached the immortality age yet.*

As the vision faded, I noticed Evander was no longer listening to the little boy but staring at me. I leaned down face to face with the little boy.

"Have you heard about me?" I asked him.

He took a step back from me. "Did I do something wrong?"

I wet my lips. "Do you like to play on the rocks next to the waterfall?"

He looked at Evander and then me.

Evander commanded, "Answer her, Kory."

The little boy's bottom lip wobbled, but he nodded anyway.

"It's very dangerous there. You can't go there anymore. Do you understand?"

He nodded again, but I don't think he understood how serious I was.

Evander said, "You love Marri, don't you?"

The little boy's eyes lit up. "Thank you so much for giving her to me. She's a beautiful pet."

Evander smiled. "I'm glad. And are you taking good care of her?"

"Of course I am," the little boy said as he puffed out his chest.

"If you go to the waterfalls or play on the rocks, I will take Marri from you and give her to another child that doesn't play on the rocks. Do you understand?"

"Yes, sir."

Evander jerked his chin. "Now go play anywhere but there."

In silence we watched Kory run off. I would have been a fool not to notice that the warriors' motions had slowed down. Obviously they had terrific hearing and were currently making their own assumptions over the conversation.

Evander slowly stood and pulled me up along with him. Never once letting go of my hand, we walked past the battling warriors and down a flowery path.

"As amazing as the warriors are," he said, "they didn't just save Kory's life."

I didn't say anything as we continued our trek through the garden. I sidestepped one nasty-looking flower, causing him to laugh.

"I promise you that they recognize that you are a friend and will not eat you. No matter how tasty they think you might be."

My eyes narrowed on the pale pink petals. "Yeah, well just in case, I think I'll give the nice flowers some distance."

His next words took me by surprise. "You haven't asked about your mate today."

Huh? "Oh, how's um…"

"Calhoun," he said with a full-blown grin.

"Don't smirk. I don't even remember my name."

His smile dropped. "But you will."

He pulled me up a small trail, and immediately I saw the waterfall from my earlier vision. "This is where I saw Kory playing."

He nodded.

"I see why he would want to come here," I said.

"Yes, but those rocks do get slippery. I'll post a guard here during the day just to make sure Kory and his friends don't get any ideas of doing something reckless."

That was sweet. I'm not sure if most people would go the extra mile to protect others. I didn't know if I was a good judge of character or not, but my gut was telling me that this warrior, though deadly, had a kind heart. Did those two things even go together?

"After you are done working out whatever it is you're thinking of, come sit on this boulder."

The huge flat space was dry and not near the waterfalls, so as soon as he let go of my elbow, I sat cross-legged. He sat in front of me. "We are going to work on controlling the visions you have. Then we are going to give you a break by switching tactics. We are going to work on your ability to communicate with others."

I frowned. "I can't communicate with others. I just hear their loud voices in my head."

"I think you can communicate with others, you just don't know how to. The voices that you hear—you can open or close that line."

My jaw dropped open as hope filled me. "How do you know if you aren't a psychic?"

"I might not be psychic, but I know a lot about fae powers, and psychics come from the fae side."

"Can we start with learning how to shut off the switchboard?" I said. "I need a giant 'Do Not Disturb' signal blasted out after five o'clock Eastern Standard Time and on weekends. Not to be a brat, but maybe holidays too."

His lips twitched. "We will see what we can do. The quicker you learn to open yourself up to your powers, the sooner you can leave here." He grabbed both of my hands in his. "When you hear voices, is it someone trying to have a direct connection with you?"

"One lady in particular, Ariana, speaks directly to me. Others I hear, but it's like their thoughts are being shoved at me."

"So this Ariana is powerful. She knows how to control the voices. The others...I'm assuming you are eavesdropping on their thoughts." His eyes narrowed on my face. "If you can control what and when you hear something, you will be less erratic."

"I'm good with less erratic."

"Close your eyes and let's begin. I want you to imagine a well of power at your center."

"I don't really have power. Not in that sense."

"The first step is to realize that you do, in fact, have power, you just need to harness it better. Now, do as I say. Imagine your power deep down inside of you."

I took a deep breath. "Now what?"

"Think of opening the power up. Bit by bit."

I pictured a tight ball that was like a head of lettuce and I peeled back layer after layer. Until each layer was completely open. "I feel no different."

"Patience," he said as his palms heated. "I want to lend you some of my power. It will run through your veins and help you to release your own."

Before I could say anything, I felt a warmth run across my palms and up my arms around my elbows and travel to my shoulders. It made its way over every inch of me.

"Picture that well of power that you've opened up spreading everywhere you feel the warmth from my power."

I shifted in my seat. His power felt magical, and here I was imagining mine looked like a head of lettuce. I wondered if I should start over.

"Focus, please."

I grumbled as I focused on the leaves of power that lay open. Mentally, I sent each piece in different directions. Trying to chase his power. Soon I felt energized. More alert than I had in a long time.

Evander's deep voice penetrated my happy thoughts. "I want

you to try to pick up my thoughts. Focus on the power spread throughout your body. From your toes to your fingertips."

I pushed my power to him and heard, "*Can you hear me? You still haven't asked about your mate.*" I could almost hear the laughter with his last thought.

Eyes still closed I said, "Yes. And what's up with all these questions about my mate?"

There was a small laugh. "I didn't ask that out loud."

My eyes popped open, and I instantly felt the power snap close into the center of my stomach.

"Did you lose control?" he asked.

I nodded. "All the lettuce came back to the salad bowl."

He arched a brow but didn't ask any questions. "Again."

I sighed but closed my eyes. It was then that I realized that I had heard his voice before. I couldn't remember what he had said, but I was certain I remembered that sexy baritone being shoved into my brain.

"Focus," he said again.

I took a deep breath. This time I pictured a diamond. It didn't work. So I went back to my head of lettuce. Patiently I pulled back each leaf and then sent the magic out to every part of my being. We did this so long that the sun faded in the sky, and I grew tired.

"Now," he said, "focus on the winter court. It's high in the mountains. See if you can get any visions about the army of the Winter King."

My brows furrowed as I concentrated. I was not coming up with anything. My legs started to bounce, and Evander reached out and placed his palms on my knees. Shocked by his touch, I stilled, and that's when the vision came to me. Evander was in black cargo pants and nothing else. He strode toward me like a predator that had just caught a glimpse of his prey—and he was starving. His hair was damp, and his skin was glistening. I breathed raggedly as the vision continued. His calloused hands reached out and snagged my waist, dragging me roughly toward him. My body flushed as his head dipped toward mine. The vision wavered, and I fought to hold on to it, but it was a lost cause.

My breaths were coming in deep as another vision swam to the surface. This time it was of the fae prince. His blond hair was spiked up, and there was a look of rage on his face. My eyes flicked open to see honey-colored eyes looking back at me. What had just happened? Did I cheat on the fae prince? Did he see the way Evander held me in his arms? Future me was a hoe. I had to put a stop to this.

"What did you see?" he asked.

I wet my lips. I knew he could sniff out a lie, so I went with a partial truth. "I had angered the fae prince. He was looking at me with—pure rage."

Evander removed his hands from my knees and sat back a little. "Maybe your thoughts were going toward him."

He sounded disappointed, probably because I wasn't able to help him.

I was about to apologize when he said, "Let's get you back to the cabin."

I wasn't sure if my pale cheeks flushed easily or not, so I looked up at the stars in hopes that he would too.

It was beautiful in this land. What if this man truly healed me? What if I was able to gaze at the stars at night and remember my name? What if I was able to remember enough to change my future so that I didn't piss off my fated mate?

"Beautiful."

"Yeah," I said, "it is."

I looked at Evander, but he wasn't looking at the sky, he was looking at me with a smile. The way his smile grew, I knew the answer to my question.

"Thank you for working with me on controlling the voices."

"You are welcome. Though my reasoning is purely selfish. I want your power to grow. In order to do that, I need you to be sane."

At least we were both on the same team. I wanted to be sane too. "Will we work on controlling the visions too?"

He stood up. "Unfortunately, you'll never be able to control the visions, but you will learn to be more accepting of them. If you don't fight what is coming to you, but instead embrace it with your power, it will not damage you further."

I looked at him then. He stretched a hand out to me, and I took it as he helped me to my feet. "Well, that's something."

He dropped my hand. As we started to walk back, I was practically touching him because I was terrified the flowers wouldn't recognize their ol' pal in the dark and they would eat me. Was that crazy thinking? Maybe, but if the straight jacket fits, tie it in the back and wear it.

"Calhoun makes the voices stop."

He was quiet for a moment. "All the high fae, the royalty, are extremely powerful. Part of his power must be blocking out what others are broadcasting to you."

"Then he probably is my other half."

He stopped walking then and turned to me. "First, you are whole, with or without a mate. Second, why would you want to be with someone, mate or not, if they block your gift?" Before I could explain, he said, "I get that you are tired. I'm not going to lie. There aren't many psychics because most of them fade from this world from premature burnout. You could take the easy way out, pick a mate that quiets the voices, or you could embrace them and help the world. Help kids like Kory."

We started walking again, and I was trying to process everything he'd said. "How do I embrace the visions?"

"The same way as you try to hear thoughts. Uncurl your power and let it be a part of you instead of suppressing it."

"If I do that," I asked, genuinely curious, "would I be picking up on stray thoughts all the time?"

"Not unless you concentrate on the person you are trying to pick up from."

As the trail narrowed, he held my hand. I realized that his eyesight was far superior to mine as he helped me down the path.

"If I remember any of this tomorrow, I'll consider what you have said."

He chuckled. "I will be healing you every chance I get. You will remember this tomorrow."

As he spoke, I could feel his magic warming my palm. "Won't you ever grow tired?"

"I just might be one of those high fae I told you about."

My eyes quickly darted to him, even though I couldn't make out his facial features on the darkened path. At the bottom of the trail we walked through the garden, and I realized that we were almost back to the cabin. A vision came so quickly that I didn't remember collapsing and strong arms grabbing me before I hit the dirt. I didn't remember being carried to the cabin. All I remembered was Evander's flesh being boiled from his body.

CHAPTER 10

"Do you want to tell me what happened?"

I blinked my eyes open and sat up on the couch.

Fatty jumped onto my lap. "Oh, Nuts! Your nose was bleeding, and your head was rolling back and forth. I thought we were going to have to call an exorcist. Again, a little disappointed that we didn't have to, but glad to have you back, crazy!"

I scratched his head. "Love you too."

"I really hate your pet demon," Evander said.

The cat purred. "Thin line between love and hate, baby."

A murderous rage came over Evander's face, but before he could kill my cat, I said, "Let me tell you what I saw."

"You still remember it?" Fatty asked.

"Sort of. I tried to open my head of lettuce, but I had too much self-doubt. Long story short, the vision came in blips, and then mingled with other visions, so I'm a little confused." I wet my lips and laid my pounding head back on the couch. "There will be a dinner tomorrow night." I turned to Evander. "You've made a lot of people angry, but they don't know that it's you they should be angry with." My hand went to my throat. "It has to do with the collars and people going missing." I didn't mention that I would be dragged away from the event by two soldiers nor that I would be thrown into a cell with my mate. I needed more information before I gave that up freely. Plus, I was worried that it would mess up timelines.

Evander sat down on the small coffee table in front of me. His knees brushed mine. "Are you not telling me something that I need to know?"

Knowing that he would recognize a lie, I replied, "Some timelines are meant to be changed. When that happens, I have this urgency. This nagging inside of me that won't relent until I have accomplished what I was born to do." I rubbed my forehead. "Other times, it's a sense of peace. In those moments I know that I need to stand by and let things play out naturally. For example, I know that I need to be at that dinner tomorrow. It's part of my timeline." I opened my eyes to look at him. "Just like I know that I can't change your timeline. When you're captured, you will go of your own free will. I saw what they were doing to you and your conditions. What I didn't understand was why you would willingly go. The only thing I can think of is they took someone you love. But regardless, it's part of your timeline."

He cocked his head to the side but didn't say anything.

"But does he die?" the cat asked without any sadness in his voice.

I shook my head. "I didn't see his death, but that doesn't mean anything."

I could have sworn the cat looked disappointed.

My eyes found Evander's as a pit developed in my stomach. "One more thing...whoever captures you has the same ability as you do. They can make flesh melt with a touch."

"Just great!" the cat said. "There are two of them."

I waited for Evander to ask questions that would possibly help him escape his captors, but instead he stood. "I'm going to go take a quick shower. Until you learn to unite with your power, the visions will hurt you," he said as he handed me a tissue for my nose. "Don't fight it. Meet the visions with your power."

When he was out of the room, Fatty came to sit next to me. "So that was intense."

"Yeah." I rubbed a palm over my heart. I didn't understand why Evander would allow someone to torture him. Was I sure that he was allowing it? No, but I was almost positive.

Fatimah asked, "How did today go?"

I caught him up on everything that had happened, then laid my head back on the soft cushions and closed my eyes. Today had been exhausting. I heard the bathroom door open, but I didn't want to move.

Fatty hissed, then in an overdramatic voice he said, "You just lay there. I'll give you a play-by-play."

"Huh?" I mumbled.

"White towel. The soft cotton would be big on most but looks tiny draped across the masculine frame of the assassin that is currently glaring at me. He's shaking his head, and water just flung from his thick mane of black hair to his muscular chest that is bronzed either from some kickass genetics or the sun. Do fae bronze in the sun? Who cares? Is he flexing his eight-pack for me, or are his abdominals just that well-formed? I bet he has lots of fae babies across the globe. Whoops, he's walking now—no, *strolling* into the bedroom. His trapezoids are huge and tight under the scrutiny of a demon."

A door slammed with such force my eyes flicked open. Slowly I turned my head to take in the cat, who had two paws resting on the back of the couch. He dropped down to all fours before he curled into a ball.

"Show's over," he said.

"Oooh you made him mad."

"Have you seen him when he's mad? The jaw was clenched. His hands were in fists. I mean, it was hotness overload. Besides, he's not going to kill me as long as he needs you."

The door opened, and Evander walked to the front of the couch wearing gray sweats and a black T-shirt. He extended a hand to me, helping me to my feet. His eyes cut to the cat. "You overestimate your worth." Then he pulled me along. "You need to sleep."

I crawled into his bed with a smile on my face. The cat really was pushing his luck. I didn't need to reach out with my powers to know what Evander was thinking. He wished he would have ended him the moment he met him.

I turned on my side and yawned as the lamp flickered off. I wanted him to heal me, but I wasn't sitting up to do it. I needed a good sleep. He didn't say a word as he lay down behind me. His body fit so perfectly with mine that I was asleep within minutes. From my vision I knew that tomorrow was going to be physically draining, so I wouldn't take a peaceful night of healing and sleep for granted.

CHAPTER 11

That morning I woke to no Evander and no Fatty. I ate some fruit and then used my power like Evander had tried to teach me. I clearly saw Fatty in the garden pouncing on something. I let the vision fade before my fruit came back up. Hopefully he wasn't eating something cute and furry. The most important thing was learning to take control of what I did or didn't see. All day I would work on keeping my gift flowing through me like a live wire. More of my memories came back and I was overjoyed. I remembered more friends' faces and their names. I wrote down a few notes and then stuffed them in my purse. Just in case.

Before dinner tonight, I wanted to try to use my gift to contact Ariana. After a quick shower, I changed into some clothes that Evander had set out for me and climbed onto the freshly made bed. I propped myself up with pillows and closed my eyes. I repeated Ariana's name like a mantra in my head as I circulated my power throughout my body. It took everything I had not let the power collapse when I heard her response.

"I see that you are getting help with your powers. That's fantastic. Push yourself and see if you can find me. Picture me."

I rubbed my sweaty palms on the borrowed pants and searched for her face. I was shocked when I saw a beautiful woman in her mid-fifties with long, black hair and brown eyes. Um...that was definitely not the Ariana that I remembered from my sleep last night. Clearly I had made a mistake. I started to back out, but her voice stopped me.

"Didn't recognize me, did you?"

"Ariana?"

She smiled, and I was mesmerized. "Ugh, I don't mean to be rude, but this isn't how I remember you."

She sat on a chaise lounge, her dainty frame looking even smaller with all the cushions surrounding her. "You're more sane than the last time we talked."

I didn't remember the last time so I said, "I saw glimpses of you last night while my memory was being restored and—"

"Right because Evander is healing you."

"Yes, and anyway you, um, no offense looked a million years old."

"Well I *am* old, but the fae world healed me just like it's healing you." She must've read my face because she said, "Don't get me wrong, Evander is doing all the heavy lifting, but being in the fae world will help undo the damage that the visions have done."

I guess that made sense. "You're here?"

"I was. Now I'm somewhere different."

Well that wasn't cryptic at all. She tilted her head to the side, and a sly smile came upon her face. "What are you trying not to think about?"

I was thinking that just by looking at her, she should have come to the fae world a long time ago.

She laughed. "You're broadcasting, dear."

"Sorry," I mumbled.

"You realize that even though I'm extremely old, I wasn't born immortal. You are not immortal. Everyone you love will eventually have to say goodbye to you unless your fated mate claims you."

What the hell did that mean?

Again she laughed. "I chose to look a certain way, let my body become broken because I was hiding from a certain male fae." At that moment, a man walked into the room and stood behind the chaise lounge. He looked about sixty and had shiny, gray hair that hung past his shoulders. He stroked his silvery beard, and his blue eyes twinkled with amusement.

"Jolene, I've heard so much about you. It's nice to meet you."

"That's my name?"

His smile dropped. Ariana waved a hand dismissively. "Your friends call you Jo, and yes it's your name." Then she tilted her head back to look at the man. "Don't fret, love, everything is going according to plan." He lovingly patted her shoulder, and her eyes found mine once again. "I was just telling Jo that even though I'm thousands of years old, I don't normally look like it."

The man laughed. "She was mad at me. Thought she could hide out on Earth with a different version of herself and I wouldn't find her."

"But you did," I said.

"I did. She is stubborn but she's the love of my life."

My eyes widened. "You're mates?" He nodded. "And um, did you claim her?"

He smiled widely at me and nodded again.

Ariana gave me a wink. "Okay enough about us. Now that you have sought me out, I need to remind you of who you are. Let me show you a vision of the past." I watched as she held up one hand and an image of me flickered before my eyes. The vision was silent, but I could tell I had been laughing. I caught an arrow with one hand and then minutes later I disappeared in a cloud of black swirls.

My mouth dropped open. Those kinds of reflexes were more of what I would associate with a vampire. "I can teleport?"

She closed out the image. "It's not teleportation, per se. It's more that you can ride the fae lines."

"Because I come from the fae side?"

She nodded.

"But not all fae can do that, can they?"

"Just the high fae."

"I'm one of the royals?"

"No, you're not a pure blood, but you're powerful. The courts would probably accept you, but they won't ever treat you fairly. That's if you choose to belong to one."

"Why would I do that?"

She gave me a small smile. "You are at your best when you are helping others. I know it doesn't seem like it right now, but it's true. The fae realm needs someone like you."

I arched my brow. "Don't they have you, though?"

She looked up at the man towering over her. "No. For thousands of years I avoided the one person that could bring me joy. Now, I'm retired. I want to be lazy and lounge around with the fae king."

My eyes widened. "You're not the fae prince's grandfather, are you?"

He smiled warmly at me. "I am."

I bit my lip. Should I tell him that his grandson is in a dungeon right now?

As if seeing my unease, he said, "Don't worry. Ariana has caught me up on all his doings. I promise you that a few nights in a cell won't harm him."

"You're mad at him?" I asked. "Even after all these years?"

"Pissed," the fae king said. "He ran from his home instead of coming to me and letting me help him. I love that boy, and that will never change, but I'm mad that he didn't think he could come to me."

That made sense in a weird, familial kind of way.

"Jo," Ariana said, bringing my attention back to her, "in a way you are a lot like Calhoun. Don't run from the ones who love you when you feel as if you made a mistake."

I had no clue what she was talking about.

"I need you to understand something," she added. "We... psychics aren't meant to intervene with every timeline. Sometimes fate will step in and stop us if it knows that we are going to change someone's fate and it wasn't meant to be."

"Um, okay?"

She gave me a smile. "Don't be too hard on yourself."

I nodded.

"And one more thing. Crazy always gets overlooked. Ride out

the crazy and you manage to sneak under the radar." She gave me a wink, and then the connection was lost.

I stretched back on the bed with a smile on my face. Maybe the cat was right and I was a lot more badass than I thought. I would take Ariana's advice to heart and hopefully get the king of badassery some of the answers he craved.

CHAPTER 12

"I don't understand how someone that looks like a villain, has psychic powers like a villain, and smells like sin can pick out clothes for you that don't involve leather and cutouts for certain body parts."

I smoothed down the cotton dress I was wearing thanks to Evander. The man in question marched toward the cat and picked him up by the scruff, throwing him out of the cabin. It wasn't until the door was shut that he took a deep breath. He really wanted to kill the cat and his restraint was admirable.

"So," he said, "run this by me one more time."

"I talked with Ariana today. From the memories I've recovered, she is my teacher and I'm her apprentice. She has instructed me in a way to keep up the crazy act, which wasn't an act a few days ago." I sighed deeply. "I guess I'm more of a liability if people know that I actually can predict the future. All I'm saying is I don't need to go around reading people's fortunes."

There was a knock on the door, and Evander opened it. I half-expected to see my cat shooting him the bird. Instead, a man that I immediately recognized stood on the other side. His blonde hair was swooped and styled to the side. Even though he wore his customary black T-shirt and cargo pants like all the other soldiers, he looked dashing.

I stood from the couch with a bright smile. "Shay! How are you feeling?"

"Alive," he said with a bashful smile. "Thanks to you."

Evander crossed his arms over his chest. "Why are you here instead of resting and continuing to heal?"

"I'm tired of laying around. Besides, there is a huge dinner tonight and I was wondering…" He shuffled his feet. "I was wondering if…"

"Spit it out, man," Evander snapped.

"I was wondering if I could escort our new guest to the dinner?" Shay said.

For several seconds Evander didn't move. Didn't say a word. Finally, he nodded and then turned to me. "Is that something you would want?"

"Jolene," I said.

Both men raised their brows at me.

"I remember my name."

"Jolene," Evander repeated the name, rolling it off his tongue in a way that sent shivers down my spine.

I cleared my throat. "But I'm told my friends call me Jo."

"So, Jo, can I send my sister to help you get ready? She's about the same size as you and she is equally grateful that you've saved me. After you're finished getting ready, I'd really like to escort you to dinner."

I gave him a bright smile. "I would love that."

He gave me a wide grin that split his face. Then he turned to talk with Evander about some scouting in Fox Run. He gave me another friendly wave before making his exit. Evander went to his room and came back out with a bag.

"That was incredibly nice of him," I mused out loud.

Evander snorted. "Yeah it has nothing to do with your beauty or that he thinks he has a chance."

"I'm practically a married woman."

He arched his brow. "Yeah, to what's his name, right?"

Dang. What was his name?

"I'll go get ready somewhere else so you have the whole cabin to yourself," Evander said.

I frowned. "You don't have to do that."

He adjusted the bag in his hand. "If a vision comes, send your power out to meet it. Eventually your power will be coursing through your body just like oxygen, but until we get there, really concentrate on getting it to relax and flow."

I gave him a nod.

"I'll see you at dinner."

Three minutes after he left, I was still standing in the same spot. Fatty was staring at me without saying anything. Finally he piped up. "Why do you look sad?"

"Why do I *feel* sad?"

There was another knock on the door. I ran to it and swung it open. Whoever I was expecting on the other side was not who was currently smiling at me—and the best part was that I remembered her.

"Vanka?"

She gave me a bright smile before setting down the items she had in her hands and throwing her arms around me. "I hoped we would meet again but I never imagined it would be because you saved my brother."

I pulled back gently. "Shay's your brother?"

She shook her head. "Yes, my favorite brother and I would have been utterly lost without him." She scooped up the bags on the floor. "I need to get you ready. We only have two hours and we have so much to talk about."

She kicked the demon out, then she sat me down at a kitchen table and started pulling my thick hair every which way until she finally decided how she wanted to style it. She was full of stories about her childhood and the warriors and Evander. She sounded as if she might have a little crush on the intimidating man, and to be honest, I couldn't blame her. He was gorgeous. After applying my makeup, she had me step into a shimmery black gown that looked like it had been poured over my small frame. I was worried that it would make me look too skinny, but when she pushed me in front of the bedroom mirror, I smiled. Somehow I managed to pull off the look. All I needed were shoes. Vanka thrust my black boots at me with a smile.

"How did you get these?" I asked.

"Evander got them for you." She lifted her leg and shook her foot at me. "You see these bad boys? They are huge. None of my shoes would fit your feet. Plus, Evander thought you would be happy to see your boots again."

I silently wondered how many people he killed when he went back through the warehouse to retrieve my boots. I slid them on and then let the dress fall back to the ground. You couldn't see the shoes, but I knew they were there. Every woman needed a good pair of shitkickers.

There was a knock at the door, and she gave me a wink. "Go answer it. It's probably Shay. I'll clean up here, get dressed, and then I'll meet you at dinner."

"Thanks, Vanka." As I made my way across the living room, a vision started to form. Instantly I reached out with my powers. Flashes came to me, and when the vision was done, I lightly touched my nose. No blood. I smiled to myself. I was healing and I was learning.

Vanka was talking but I just nodded, not actually catching the last part of her sentence.

Hoping she hadn't noticed that I wasn't listening, I said, "Thanks again."

"No, thank you for saving me and my brother. I'll never be able to repay you."

"Meh. Consider it repaid."

She was laughing as I opened the door to see her brother on the other side.

His smile dropped as he let out a low whistle. "Wow, you're absolutely gorgeous."

I patted him on the arm before exiting the cabin. "Let's see if you still say that when I start talking to people you can't see."

There was an elegant carriage right out front with magnificent black horses that looked the size of dragons. Shay nodded to the driver, then gave me a boost up the steps.

"Even though it's a short distance, Evander didn't want you to walk. He said you might not be able to sit on a horse in a tight dress."

"How did he know that my dress would be tight?" I asked as Shay settled in next to me. He hit the roof twice, and the driver pulled the horses onto the narrow road.

He gave me a strange look. "He picked it out."

He grimaced as he leaned back against the cushions, and a flicker of pain filtered across his face.

"You're still not feeling a hundred percent, are you?"

He shook his head. "They injected me with iron. Evander healed me as much as he could, but it's up to my body to do the rest." He turned to look at me. "I want to deeply thank you for rescuing me."

I didn't respond because I knew something else was on his mind.

"Evander has done so much for me. He took me in when no one else would. I'd like to return the favor. Evander told me that you had seen his capture?"

I nodded.

"He also said that you believed it didn't come to him as a surprise."

Again I nodded.

"That means someone will take one of us. He would knowingly walk into a trap if it meant sparing one of his friends."

"I think I know what you're asking, but honestly the visions sort of control me at the moment."

He dipped his head as he rested his forearms on his legs. "Evander had said that you are working on using your power. I know he wants everyone to think you're crazy and I promise I won't tell anyone anything differently, but tonight if you could please try to pick up on anything pertaining to Evander and why he might willingly get captured, I'd be doubly in your gratitude."

I patted his knee. "Okay. I'll do my best. Oh, and Shay?"

He quirked a brow. "Yes."

"You want to repay me for saving your life?"

"Of course. I'll do anything."

I gave him a warm smile. "Great! When I get arrested tonight, let me go. Don't put up a fight."

"You're going to get arrested?" he said in horror. "I'll tell Evander."

I shook my head as I gently laid an arm on his shoulder. "Please don't say a word to anyone. If you do, it changes the timeline, and I try not to do that if no one is getting harmed."

"Getting arrested isn't harmful?"

I scrunched my brow. "Well, actually I didn't see what happened after I was delivered to the cell, but I'm not worried."

"You're not?"

"Not in the least." The carriage had come to a stop, but Shay remained unmoving, just staring at me. I shooed him with my hand. "Let's go have some fun."

Shay escorted me into the castle and through the halls, making sure he didn't walk too fast and keeping an eye on me. People stopped to stare, but we ignored them both. Right before we entered the ballroom, I stopped him by grabbing his arm.

"What's wrong?" he asked.

Another vision—this time of a pretty brunette—flashed in my mind. She wasn't high fae. No, she would be working tonight... serving for the high fae.

I looked up at Shay. "Am I bleeding?"

He looked at me strangely. "No."

"Great. I'm on a roll. So listen, big guy, I know that the whole 'being arrested' thing made you a little nervous, but finding your true mate is a big deal, right?"

Hesitantly he said, "Yes." Then more forcefully he added, "Of course."

"Of course it is. I have a mate, you know."

"You do?"

Obviously I had an issue with names. "Yeah, um, the fae prince. You know, the one locked up in the cells."

His mouth dropped in shock. "Calhoun?"

I dropped his arm and clapped. "Yes! Calhoun. I knew that was his name. Anyway, your mate will be coming through the big doors next to the kitchen after the band starts playing. Do yourself a favor and speed up your timeline by three years and stop her for an hors d'oeuvre. I promise your conversation with her will be better than the finger food itself."

"Are you serious?"

"About the mate or your food?"

He gave me a toothy grin. "You're the best."

With one hand on my back, he escorted me into the room. People were sitting at tables everywhere, and along the back wall some were standing and engrossed in conversations. A pair of honeyed-colored eyes met mine from across the room. Evander did a slow gaze down my body and back up to my face, then his eyes moved over to Shay. He gave the fae a nod before turning back to the tall, gorgeous blonde he was talking with.

"Does Evander know that you have found your mate?"

I watched with a frown as the blonde tilted her head back and laughed at something Evander had said.

"Yep."

Shay was talking, but I wasn't paying attention. I was watching the decked-out blonde in the killer red dress flirting shamelessly with Evander.

"So you're okay if I just leave you here?"

My head jerked to Shay once I realized that I hadn't been listening. "Of course! Your fated mate is going to be walking through that door any second." I gave him a slight push. "Go. And try to be charming."

He gave me a wink. "I'll see what I can muster up."

I stood there for a few more seconds before something warm wound itself around my leg.

I looked down to see my cat purring. A few of the fae looked over at us and snarled.

"What are you doing here?" I asked.

"I wanted to see what the big dinner was all about."

I smiled at a grumpy-looking woman who was giving us the death stare. "We're definitely not making friends."

"Screw 'em. Who needs them? I'm going to go check out the dessert table. I'll be right back."

"Please be careful," I said. "They really don't like the fact that a demon is in their safe place."

"We're literally in the slums and they think they are better than us?" He hissed at a nearby fae as he strolled across the ballroom floor like he owned the place. My cat might be crazier than me.

I looked back to where Evander had been standing only to discover that he was gone. A warm hand pressed into my back, and I instantly leaned into it, knowing that my night was going to be all crap.

CHAPTER 13

"Where's your date?" Evander asked as I turned toward him.

"I sent him over there," I said, jerking my thumb over my shoulder. "His fated mate will be walking through that door any second, carrying less than desirable appetizers."

His lips twitched. "I'll have to make sure to offer him congratulations or maybe condolences."

I frowned. "Why?"

"Well he did give up the prettiest girl in the room."

"Oh, I bet you get all the girls." I fanned myself. "That face with those scary one-liners you dole out."

He cocked his head to the side. "You like my threats more than my flirting?"

Was he flirting? I mean, I was practically hitched to a fae prince and what a stupid question. "There is no comparison to your scary slogans." I elbowed him in the side as I turned so we were facing the same direction. "And you can't flirt with me."

I could feel him looking down at me. "And why is that?"

"Because, like your friend, I have a mate." When he didn't say anything, I looked up at him. "What?"

"Calhoun?"

"Um…who else?"

He put his hands in his pockets. "What color eyes does he have?"

Was this man serious? I barely remembered the fae prince's name. When I didn't say anything, he asked, "If you had to give a missing person's description of him, could you?"

"Of course I could. He's got a cute face, blond, and is somewhere between..." Dang I forgot his height. "He's tall."

He smirked down at me. "Most fae from the summer court fit that description."

I rolled my eyes. He asked if I could give a description. He never said it had to be a *good* one. He ran a hand through his hair, and I immediately knew something was wrong by the tension in his shoulders.

I looked at the food spread across the long adjoining tables and the fae in their pretty dresses and accessories. "What's wrong?" I asked.

"There are people starving in the surrounding villages, and yet we have a feast before us." He put one hand on my back and steered me farther into the room. Huge lanterns hung on the walls behind the rows of tables, casting a golden hue on the shiny floors of the castle.

"So why all the food?"

"One of the Winter King's mistresses is visiting."

"The slums?" I coughed out. "But why?"

"That's a question I was hoping you could answer," he said. "I have a feeling as to why, but there's no concrete evidence. There has been tension between myself and the Winter King." My brows rose in question. "The winter court decided to stop killing criminals and instead turn them loose in this No Man's Land that sits between all the courts. Then the winter court decided that the lower fae were draining them of their food and supplies since they didn't bring a whole lot to the kingdom and the king decided to banish them here."

"To live with the criminals?"

He nodded at someone who waved to us from across the room. "Yes. There has been a war waging between the lawless fae and the powerless fae ever since."

I took in his handsome profile. His clothes weren't as fancy as some of the fae flitting around. He had calluses on his hands and muscles that insinuated that he worked out a lot. His cabin was small, but I could tell that people respected him, so he must have some sort of authority here in the No Man's Land. I'd seen his power, so the real question was, was Evander a criminal?

He turned to me. "I see someone that I need to go talk to. I'm going to sit you here at this table. Don't move." He gave me a stern look. "And don't eat or drink anything that I haven't personally given you. If you get an opportunity to dive into the mistress's head, do so. I would be surprised if she is thinking of the information that I need, but it's worth a shot."

I saluted him. His eyes narrowed. Guess he didn't think I was as funny as I did. He ushered me to the table and pulled out a chair for me. I sat at the empty table and smiled at all the eyes that drifted my way.

"I'll be right back."

After he walked toward the opposite end of the huge ballroom, I focused on my power. Again I tried something relatively cooler than a head of lettuce, but when my power fizzled out, I went back to the vegetable. I pushed my power out to each part of my body just like Evander had instructed. My intention was to control any visions that came my way. I wanted to know who was responsible for the future kidnapping of a man I was really starting to admire. My power reached out into the crowd of seventy or so fae. My goal was never to eavesdrop on anyone's private thoughts, even though that's exactly what happened.

My concentration was broken when a striking woman with blonde hair pulled out the chair beside me and sat down. Even sitting, she was so tall that I felt like a child next to her. Her hair was luscious and wavy. Her skin was flawless, and her lips were painted a ruby red.

"Hi," she said with a Cheshire grin. "I'm Alexis. I've heard so much about you."

My eyes flickered to the matching ruby-red collar that she wore around her neck and then back up to her eyes.

Earlier I had accidentally clamped on to her thoughts, and now I could hear her as if she were speaking out loud. It was a wonder that my power didn't close in on itself or that I showed no reaction to her.

"Nice to meet you," I replied. Not wanting to give her my real name, I added, "I'm Nuts."

A look of disgust colored her face before she quickly removed it. She signaled to someone, and a waiter came over and handed her two glasses of wine. I had to hand it to her. I never saw the vial up her sleeve. That was how good she was. Thankfully the vision I had earlier would save my life tonight. She pushed a glass to me and then picked up her own and took a small sip. Her eyes landed on my untouched wine and then back on me.

"Are you not going to take a drink?"

"Oh, well Evander has asked me to not drink or eat while I'm here," I said sweetly.

She laughed. "Oh, and do you listen to everything men tell you to do?" She set her cup down. "I sat here because you looked like the most interesting person in this boring place, but I can see that I was mistaken."

I silently wondered if that patronizingly—bordering on bullying—tactic she used worked on most. When she didn't vacate her seat, I realized that no matter her tone, she wasn't going to give up that easily.

I nodded over to Evander. "Who is that woman he is talking to?"

The moment she turned to see Evander escort a pretty brunette out of the ballroom, I switched the glasses.

"Why, are you jealous?" she asked as she turned back to face me.

I pulled my newly switched wine glass closer to me, and her eyes lit up with anticipation.

"What's up with the collar you're wearing?"

Her hand flew to the item in question. "I heard you were suffering from burnout from your inability to control your visions, but you can't pick up on anything can you?"

Knowing better then to lie, I lifted one shoulder in a half-shrug. Then my eyes drifted back over to Evander, wondering what he would do in this position. The stunning woman tracked my gaze.

"The Winter King is highly suspicious of him." She must have seen the confusion on my face. Reaching out, she patted my hand with false sincerity as she said, "Us girls have to stick together. He's ruthless. Forget him." She gave me one last pat. "Sometimes Feral lets us out to play. We come here to the slums for easy pickings, but a lot of the time the king's loyal servants don't make it back."

As easy as picking the strings of an instrument, I picked her thoughts. Feral was the name of the Winter King. He allowed his people to come here to the slums to blow off steam. That meant a variety of things, but usually ended with an innocent person dying. Feral thought that the people from the slums were banding together and taking down those he allowed admittance into the slums. At first he thought it was funny, but now he was getting concerned. The last group of men didn't return.

Her thoughts cut off and I frowned. I had a feeling the group who had tortured Shay were the last men to fail to return to the winter court.

"Now let's make a toast." She smiled prettily, hiding her terror that someone like me actually existed. If she ended me, she could earn bonus points with her lover. Her eyes darted to two soldiers flanking the door. Their eyes were scanning the crowd, but they weren't looking at us. The Winter King had sent her with two men loyal to him. They were extremely powerful, but even with that, she believed he should have sent a whole sentry with her just to prove how much he enjoyed her. She wasn't stupid enough to think he actually cared for her, but she didn't need his feelings. She needed his protection, his riches, his power.

I picked up my glass. "Here is to villains that try not to be bad but are left with no other options."

She frowned, but since I was doing what she needed me to do, she didn't question me. Shame.

She grabbed her glass and toasted me. "Bottoms up," she said with a smirk.

We both took large swigs from our glasses. I knew the moment she realized that she had messed up. Her eyes rounded in shock as she grabbed her collared neck with both hands. Her breathing became more and more shallow.

I sat the glass down on the table. "Maybe I am the most interesting person here."

Her eyes twitched as they tried to jerk toward mine. Foam spilled from her ruby-red lips, and seconds later her head crashed to the table. Someone screamed, and even *I* hadn't predicted what would happen next.

CHAPTER 14

Alexis' guards were before me within seconds. They didn't have proof that I had just killed their charge, but they also didn't seem to care. Shay and his sister were beside me in moments.

"Unhand her," Vanka snarled.

"We will do no such thing," the tallest one said.

The room was pure chaos. The two guards needed to get me out of the room before innocent bystanders were hurt. Also, Evander had disappeared.

I nodded. "Why don't you take me to the dungeons until you can figure out what it is you want to do with me."

The guards looked at me in confusion and then at one another.

Shay was completely quiet, but I could tell it was killing him to stand there mute. Vanka cast him a glance before she said to the guards, "If you harm her, you won't make it out of this room."

"Are you threatening us?" the other guard said.

I smiled. "It sounded like it. So, I see the future and I can tell you that her words are true. If you choose to go that route and harm me, then you'll be dead within the hour." Whether they believed me or not I didn't know, but they heard the truth in my words. That swayed them. What I didn't add was that either way they were dead.

I cleared my throat. "Your charge is dead. You need to find out who did it. I'm sure there are witnesses, but they are leaving rather quickly in the general panic. One of you should escort me, and the other should probably stay here. See if you can find any witnesses."

One of the guards gave me a funny look. "Are you saying that you didn't kill the king's mistress?"

"That's exactly what I'm saying." And I truly believed that. Alexis killed herself with her conniving ways.

One of the men grabbed me by the arm and said to the other guard, "Lock this place down. Find the murderer. I'll place this one in the dungeon for now. Even if she didn't kill the king's mistress, if she is what she says she is then the king might have a new mistress. A more powerful one at that."

Yuck. No thanks. There were things I wanted to do in life, but making out with someone named Feral wasn't one of them.

I was escorted rather quickly to the dungeons. Evander had yet to reappear. Probably somewhere more private to do less talking with the brunette. Shay looked as if he was about to intervene, but I shook my head with a smile. He turned on his heel and exited out of one of the many doors. My best guess was he was on his way to find Evander.

I always wondered what it would be like to participate in a walk of shame. This isn't exactly how I had envisioned it, though. One of the soldiers dragged me out of the ballroom. I held up my blue silk dress in one hand so that I wouldn't trip on the hem as he practically flew with me out the door. We went down several flights to the dungeons. They were every bit as cool as I thought they would be: Dark, damp, and smelling like torture.

He took me down three more steps, opened a cell, and then none too gently shoved me into it. He practically ran from the dungeon, but not because he was terrified of me. I picked up on his erratic thoughts about getting back to the mess in the ballroom. Maybe my power was completely awesome. Turning, I smiled when I saw my cellmate.

My mate said, "Well you are a sight for sore eyes. Just wish we were meeting under different circumstances."

I did a little shimmy. "Sucky circumstances, I know, but can we talk about how beautiful this dress is?"

He was slightly shaking his head as a grin came over his face. "Glad to see they didn't break your personality. You look beautiful."

"How are you faring?" I asked.

He stood up slowly and cracked his neck. "I've been better."

I chewed on my lip. "Yeah, sorry. Way to read the room, right?" I looked around the cell. "We need to get you out of here."

"Good luck with our escape, beautiful. Everything is coated in iron."

I closed my eyes and began to concentrate. My vision didn't show me what happened after I landed myself in the dungeon. I needed to look to the future and see if there was a way out of this mess.

"What are you doing?" he asked.

"I sort of have power that I can push out. I mean nothing as badass as some of the fae I've seen here, but maybe if I concentrate I can figure out a way to get on the other side of the bars. There has to be a way to escape."

I ignored his snort. When he gasped, that's when I opened one eye. Black swirls slithered up my dress and around my waist.

"Uh oh," I said. "That wasn't supposed to happen."

The black swirls covered every inch of me until I was no longer visible, only to disappear in a blink of an eye. I was standing on the other side of the cell. The fae prince and I mirrored facial expressions. Our jaws were open, and our eyes were wide as we just stood there, staring at each other. He was the first to move. He neared the bars, careful not to touch them. He reached between the bars and grabbed my hand.

"How did you do that?"

"Did I just create a portal?"

He shook his head. "That was something that I have never seen before. You moved like the grim reaper." His eyes traveled the length of my body. "Do you know what this means?"

"I'm more badass than I thought?"

"No," he said quietly. "I mean yes, but not what I meant. You can grab the keys and free me."

Voices sounded from the top of the stairs. One angry one that I happened to recognize was shouting, "Why would you put her in the cells?"

"We didn't, my lord. The king's guards escorted her here after believing that she killed Alexis."

"Why would you not immediately come to get me?" He growled, and I felt his power rolling off him before I could even see him.

With the last few steps, Evander and three of his soldiers rounded the corner. His eyes flicked to where the fae prince's hand gripped mine through the bars, then he stopped in his tracks.

"I thought you said that she was in the cell?"

A female warrior gaped at me. "I'm just as confused as you are, sir."

I pulled my hand gently from the fae prince's. "To be fair, I was actually in the cell."

Evander's eyes narrowed in on me. "Are you trying to free him?"

I looked at the keys on the wall. "I mean, well, yeah that was the plan until you all showed up."

The other female warrior looked at me with shock. "That's treason."

"Big word," I said, "for a simple task."

"Simple," Evander repeated. "How did you plan on getting him out of the castle and through the rest of No Man's Land without anyone knowing?"

I thought of my black swirly thing that literally transported me to where I wanted. If I explained it, I would seem even crazier than I was.

I lifted a shoulder. "I don't really like to make plans."

He arched his brow. "I need you to know that I would have found you wherever you had gone."

Again that could be a little creepy, but when my stomach fluttered, I realized that I might be into dominating alphas too. I sighed as I put my hands on my hips. It was becoming pretty obvious that I had a ton of personality flaws.

Boots sounded on the steps, and the guard who had escorted

me down came around the corner. He froze when he saw me out of my cell. "How did you get out?" he asked as Evander took a step closer to me.

I looked over at Evander to see how I should respond, but his eyes were on my flesh, and he had a murderous look on his face. His fingers lightly touched my arm where bruising was appearing from when the guard had grabbed me.

"I bruise easily," I said.

His fingertips gently stroked my flesh, causing goosebumps, his touch at war with his face.

His voice was low as he glared at the guard. "Did you do this?"

The king's guard scoffed. "Escort a prisoner to the cell? Yes, I did. Of course it was before we knew that the princess was killed by a faulty malfunction in her collar. Regardless I couldn't allow the main suspect to roam around the room."

When Evander took a step away from me, I winced. I didn't have a vision, but I knew what was coming. He grabbed the sword from one of his soldiers' sheaths and swung. This all happened in the blink of an eye. The guard collapsed in two pieces. The sexy villain cleaned his blade on the dead man's pants and then returned the blade to his soldier. No one moved.

He took three steps toward me and grabbed me around the waist. The breath I had been holding in came out in a rush. Yep, I was definitely into domineering and handsy too.

"And you saw all of this?" he asked.

I nodded. "Yeah, but—"

"Not another word," he said.

"Excuse me, my lord," one of the female soldiers said.

"Not another word from any of you," he boomed, and a wave of power blasted from him, pushing the warriors back several steps. "I need to talk to Jolene. Everyone out."

He didn't release me or take a step back as his soldiers left the dungeon without another word.

"Do you want to go?" Evander asked, and at first I thought he was asking me the question but then he turned his head to rake a scathing glare at the prince. "Answer me."

The fae prince wet his lips while casting me a nervous glance.

"Of course I want to be freed. I need to claim the throne in the summer court."

His hands slid from my waist, and I pressed my legs together. Here I was getting hot from a touch as my mate watched. Man, I was bad news.

Evander walked over to the keys hanging on a hook and snagged them from the hook. He unlocked the fae prince's cell and swung the door open. "Then you are freed. I'll even give you a horse if you need one. You have until sundown to leave No Man's Land."

"What happens after sundown?" I genuinely wanted to know.

"I'll melt his flesh," Evander said with a smile.

I laughed. "You are so good, my friend. So good!"

The fae prince rushed out of the cell toward me. "Come on, let's go."

I didn't move, a panicked frenzy setting in at the thought of leaving this place, and maybe even Evander. It had to be because he was healing me. That was all. Otherwise, of course I'd want to go with my mate, right?

Evander tsked. "Oh, I forgot to mention that you can go, but she has to stay."

I felt relieved that Evander was forcing me to stay. I would revisit those feelings later. Much later.

The fae prince's face was an open book, so there was no need to try to listen to his thoughts. He wanted to go. He needed to go. But to just leave me here? He didn't know if he could live with himself. He was at war...an internal battle of his wants and chivalry.

Helping him make his decision, I said, "You need to go. Claim your throne. I'll be fine here."

He cast a look at Evander and then the dead guard on the floor. "How can you trust this man?"

"He's not going to kill me. I'm too valuable."

He gave me a strange look.

"He won't. He needs me."

"Time's ticking," Evander said.

"I'll come back for you," the fae prince promised. He took a step toward me, but Evander growled, causing the fae prince to do an about-face and dart toward the steps.

"That wasn't nice," I said.

"You don't like nice," he replied as he wrapped me in his arms.

"What are you doing?"

"Escorting you to the cabin, little lamb."

One minute we were in the cell and the next we were in the cabin. I had to admit, his mode of traveling was nice, but it wasn't as cool as mine. Fatimah was on the couch when Evander let go of me.

"You will tell me everything," Evander said.

Fatimah perked up. "Oh this sounds interesting."

"Where did you go?" I asked my demon.

The cat looked miffed. "Some crazy lady in the kitchen chased me out with a broom." He was licking his paw and wiping his face, looking as if he were tending a wounded ego.

Evander looked at the cat. "If you speak again, I'll throw you out."

Fatimah looked put out, but he kept his mouth shut.

I told Evander everything that happened after Alexis sat next to me.

His brow furrowed. "She tried to kill you?"

I nodded.

His jaw was tightened with barely suppressed rage. "I smelled the poison on her glass."

Luckily it wasn't directed at me, so I gave him a moment to calm down. I ran my hands down the blue silk. It was a beautiful dress. Too bad I didn't get to show it off. When his breathing was a little steadier, I peeked up at him through my lashes. "It's true, though."

His nose flared. "Why would she want to kill you?"

"Obviously," Fatimah said, "because that Alexis chick was trying to take out the competition."

Evander's hand moved and at the same time so did Fatimah. I watched the cat go flying to the door that was wrenched open by no one. The cat yelped as he was thrown out and the door slammed behind him.

I shook my head. "That's what I'm talking about. Total badassery."

His lip twitched before he gave me a frown. "This is serious. The Winter King will want to know what happened to his mistress, and unfortunately there won't be any witnesses to tell him about her faulty collar."

"That's why I said let the timelines play out. I saw that you were going to take care of it. How did you make it look like the collar detonated?"

"I was productive with the amount of time I had."

Another T-shirt in the making. "You haven't killed the other guard yet, though?"

He shook his head.

"Good. Don't."

"Shay and Vanka said you could see the future. If one of the king's guards hears about that, he will come for you. Do you understand?"

I beamed at him. "Of course I do."

His eyes narrowed. "You told the guards on purpose, didn't you?" When I just continued to smile, he said, "Maybe you really are the Doomsayer queen."

More like doomsday but whatever.

He folded his arms over his chest, and I admired the way his suit fit him as if it was stitched onto his body. "Tell me why."

"The king is coming. We can't stop him, but if he finds value...*worth* in me, I'll be able to slow him down." I rubbed my forehead. "I'm not exactly sure yet, but from what I've seen, I might be able to save your life."

He scoffed. "That's hard to believe."

"But you do believe me, don't you?"

"Maybe, but you are an anomaly. Speaking of which, do you mind telling me how you escaped the cell?"

"This is a little harder to believe than me saving the king of badasses."

"Try me," he said dryly.

"Okay, so um, I pushed my power out like we practiced, and I was trying to think of a vision that would hopefully tell us how to get out of the cell."

"Us?"

"Yeah, me and Calhoun."

"Of course you wouldn't want to leave your mate behind," he said, his voice laced with humor and something else that wasn't as easily discernable.

I threw my hands up. "Of course. I'm a lot of things, but a leaver of mates isn't one of them. Anyway I was trying to conjure up a vision of how to escape and then these black swirls coated my whole body. Next thing I knew, I was outside of the cell."

"Same thing you did that night with the demons in the hotel!" Fatimah shouted, his paws and nose pressed to the window. "Except for you—"

I watched as the cat fell off the windowsill.

"Really hate him," Evander said. "So you can teleport in an unusual way."

I shrugged. "Guess so." I sat on the couch and crossed my legs. Evander's eyes went to the slit in my dress and stayed there for a second. He cleared his throat and his eyes slowly met mine. I ignored the yummy feeling in my belly. "I have to tell you, Evander, I'm becoming cooler and cooler every minute."

He laughed before he took a seat beside me on the couch. "One more question. Why would you leave when I'm healing you?"

I had to really think about the truth. "I never said I would leave."

His golden eyes were staring at me as if he was satisfied by my answer but he needed more. "Because you need to be healed?"

"Of course, but also because I think this is a part of my timeline." I frowned as the truth of my next words hit me. "I think I'm right where I'm supposed to be."

He studied my face as if he was trying to figure out something. His gaze was intense, and I tried not to squirm as he continued to stare. Finally he stood and stretched a hand out to me. I eyed it warily.

"Come on," he said. "Get changed. As beautiful as you look in that dress, I think you'll be more comfortable in riding pants."

"Where are we going?"

"I want you to see what it is we are doing here."

Without asking any questions, I quickly went into the bedroom to change. Another truth was I wanted to know more about this man. Who would take someone that couldn't even remember her own name and look at her like she wasn't crazy? He believed me. Maybe one day he would believe *in* me. Wouldn't that be something?

CHAPTER 15

WE TOOK ONE HORSE. HE DIDN'T GIVE ME THE OPTION OF RIDING my own. It was at that moment that I knew that Jolene, whatever my last name was, loved alphas. As he settled me in front of him, I thought that he was as possessive as he was bossy. I don't know exactly what it said about me, but I was here for it.

I sat in front of him, not even trying to keep my distance. I completely smooshed up against him, my head resting on his chest. I told myself it was because I had a crick in my neck, but the truth was I couldn't seem to stop myself from trying to get closer to him.

We were both quiet as we headed through each village that made up No Man's Land. They all looked a little different, but at their heart they were all the same. Every corner, sidewalk, and pub had equal amounts of hope and hunger. Now I understood what he meant by the food in the ballroom.

Everyone we passed either tipped their head to Evander or crossed to the other side of the street. He stopped in front of a bar with so many missing letters on the sign that I couldn't guess what the establishment was called. He jumped from the horse in one fluid motion and then helped me from the huge beast. My body slid down his, setting off a flutter in my belly. To play off my racing heart, I gave him a wink as I stepped away from him.

After tying the horse to a post, he grabbed my hand and pulled me into the bar.

It was crowded and it smelled like urine and vomit. My nose twitched and my eyes watered.

He leaned down close to my ear. "Don't worry, you'll get used to it."

Doubt it. I might forget it, but I'd never get used to it. He opened the door and walked beside me as we entered the dimly lit bar. It was so dark that I couldn't make out if the fae sitting at tables were male or female. He ushered me to a table in the back. I worked on pushing my powers out as I took a seat and prayed I didn't catch a nasty disease in the meantime.

Someone shuffled over. I could see it was a young fae girl who didn't look like she needed to be in the establishment at all. Heck, I didn't need to be in here. Without asking us what we wanted, she set down two glasses of something that splashed over the rim, adding to the already sticky table.

"So why are we here?" I asked as she walked away.

He put his elbows on the table—a bold move in this place.

"I'm not a psychic, but I have a feeling that we aren't on the same page," Evander said.

I looked around the dank room. This would be the perfect place to murder someone. Their blood would mingle with the sticky substances that seemed to coat the floor, tables, and chairs.

"Is this where you kill me?" I asked.

His brows shot up to his hairline. "No."

"Are you about to tell me that if I don't bend to your will, you will skin me like a deer and wear my hide?"

His lip twitched. "Again, no."

"Maybe you're going soft." Now I understood how the cat felt as disappointment crashed into me.

There was humor in his voice. "Still a badass."

I lifted a shoulder. "Jury's out on that one. I mean, did you melt anyone's flesh from their bones today?"

"I made someone physically look as if they had detonated. Does that count?"

I tapped a finger to my chin. "Hmm, I don't know. The first

shows control, the latter is just a burst of power. *If* you did what you said you did."

He bowed his head, whether it was in prayer or to hide his laughter was anyone's guess.

"So why are we here if not for nefarious purposes?"

He rested his chin on his fists as he continued to look at me. "I'm healing you, correct?"

I nodded.

"Good. Then you understand that you owe me and that I always collect on my debts. Now that you have sped up the process of the king coming here, I need answers."

"Technically the king doesn't come here. He sends his goons, and he was always going to send them. That timeframe never changed."

"But you will focus more on the numbers and their strategy plan?"

I started to say yes but then thought better of it. Baiting him, I leaned forward with anticipation. "Or?"

"Or I'll wear your hide like a trophy, and I must tell you that would be a complete waste." His knuckles grazed my cheek.

I leaned back in my chair with a smile. Now that was badass.

A grin melted onto his face. "We are here because I want you to unleash your powers. Help me. Find the monsters, Jolene." My name rolled from his lips in an almost sensual way.

I shivered.

I mentally slapped myself. Was I normally this distracted by a pretty face? "What monsters?"

"I think you've seen that something is amiss here in No Man's Land."

I nodded, but when he didn't elaborate, I said, "Listen, if you need my help or you need me to understand something, you aren't doing a very good job of explaining."

He leaned forward and I winced. He was definitely going to need a bleach wipe for his elbows. "Let me tell you about the Winter King. He is an evil man who likes to rule his court with terror and pain."

I nodded. "Typical villain. Give me more."

"Of course he can allure. He's fae, but he also has the ability of telepathy. Like you, he can mentally gather information from others. He can't transmit thoughts from one mind to another, though." He gave me a wicked smile. "That's where you have him beat, little lamb."

"I have a feeling he can do more, though."

"He can. Once he locks onto someone's mind, he owns them. Has complete control over them. He can't hold the person's mind for too long, though, or he'll go mad."

"Yeah, I know how that feels. Crazy is overrated. I would not recommend it."

"The Winter King has a problem on his hands. His people are having a hard time reproducing. All fae, actually, have a hard time, but the winter court has been struggling for years to reproduce. Some say it's because they are cursed. The Winter King has been commanding his people to go to the human world and use their glamor on humans to get them to fall in love with them. The purpose is to produce children. Female fae go back to the winter court as soon as they are with child, and the males impregnate a human, and then they leave the human world to show back up when the child becomes of age."

"When they come into power?"

"If. That's the downside to reproducing with humans. There's a chance that the child will have no fae powers. So, if the child has power, they bring him or her back to the winter court. If they don't, then they leave their offspring in the human world."

I was speechless. Nope. No, I wasn't. "Using glamor on humans is horrendous. All those men and women used just so that they can possibly produce offspring that may or may not develop fae power?"

"It's illegal in the other courts, and as heinous as it is, that's not the worst part. The fae who returned pregnant to the winter court…if their children have no or little fae power, they were cast out, and no other courts would take them."

Then it hit me. "He started this two hundred years ago?"

Evander nodded. "That's when No Man's Land was developed."

"They needed somewhere to go, so they settled here. Then the Winter King started sending any 'troublesome' fae here, and those fae now make up most of the soldiers. Every day they patrol No Man's Land to try to make it a safer place."

Something flittered across my mind. "His mistress Alexis wore a collar and so did her guards. I've actually seen a few fae walking around with collars around their necks. Are those the ones that are causing trouble here?"

"Yes, but recently he has been acquiring other supernaturals from different factions to be a part of his army." A table beside us got rowdy, and his eyes narrowed to slits as he studied the drunken couple. They stood and slowly stumbled through the crowded tables toward the door.

A vision came to me so quickly that everything around me faded into the background. *Two hundred years ago, the Winter King got a powerful fae pregnant. She was beautiful with raven hair to her knees and faded brown eyes. Considering that birth rates were down, the mother knew what a blessing it was to have a child that had both fae parents, but as she saw what the king was doing to her people, she knew that she couldn't let him find out that she was with child. She worried that the king would groom her baby to be evil as well, so she went to the human world and pretended to get impregnated by a human.*

As the months passed, she became more worried that the king would find out that she carried his child. Desperation kicked in, and she begged her sister who had just been cast to the new place, No Man's Land, to take her baby. Her sister had told her that the only way to fool the king would be to exchange her child for a human child, a changeling in the human world, but the mother couldn't bring herself to take away someone's child. The mother told everyone that the child died in childbirth, and she got away with it for almost fifteen years.

Careful not to touch the top of the table, I leaned closer. "The Winter King read the mother's mind, didn't he? He found out that she had lied to him."

Evander grew very still. "What did you just see, little lamb?"

I quickly retold my vision, never once ignoring the fact that he barely moved. Finally he said, "Yes. He picked up enough to know that he had fathered a child. He came here to No Man's Land and killed every child that was fifteen years old."

My mouth dropped in shock. "He wanted to kill his child?"

"He knew that the child would be powerful. He couldn't have his offspring overthrowing him one day."

Tears gathered in my eyes. "And the mother?"

Evander swallowed as his eyes dropped to the table. "He needed a description, so his plan was to torture her slowly until he caught a stray thought. His mistake was to step out of the room long enough for the mother to take her own life."

I quickly dashed away a stray tear. I hated when I was so mad that I cried. The anger inside of me for the people of No Man's Land, for the humans caught in the crossfire, and for the mother and child was unfathomable.

"So the child died along with every other kid around the same age?"

"Innocent kids died, yes, but not the child."

No longer caring about the sticky table, I put my arms on the flat surface and leaned in. "How did the child survive?"

His eyes met mine and he gave me a sad smile that had my heart dropping. "The mother's sister who was raising the child got a warning from a lady named Ariana. She ran to the human world with the child until the kid came into his powers. Then she brought him back."

When I finally closed my mouth, I said, "I'm sorry I got off topic."

He gave me a small smile. "I'm glad to see you are beginning to control your visions."

We sat there in the darkened bar, not speaking for what felt like an eternity. Finally, I asked, "Tell me about the supernaturals who wear collars. Did the Winter King do that?"

"Yes, those that wear collars belong in his army. One day you won't have to ask questions, you'll just know," he said, and almost didn't sound too pleased by the prospect.

"But until I'm at that level of power, can you answer my questions? Why do some of the fae have tattoos of a string of symbols behind their ear? It looks like a half moon at the top and then stars below it."

"The winter court's symbol is a full moon. All the high fae who have chosen their path and would never go back to the winter court have marked themselves. It's a way to identify those who are loyal to our cause. I would suggest not trusting anyone who doesn't carry that tattoo."

I filed that away for later. "And what *is* your cause?"

"The king has had an important key for hundreds of years. He sends some of his guards to different portals across the world to collect."

"Collect?"

"The king likes to find small children and bring them to the winter court."

I frowned. That didn't sound like the king he had been describing. "He was saving the children?"

He laughed without mirth. "No. He was grooming them. Molding them to be the perfect killing machines. He frees them from a portal at an early age, and then he collars them to make sure that if they ever try to escape, they die."

"Die?"

"The collars detonate."

I rubbed my forehead. I had so many questions that I didn't know where to begin. "Why are there so many kids in the portals?"

"Supernaturals who are locked in the portals can still have children."

Ugh. This king was all about taking children away from their parents.

"I see that look," Evander said. "Don't feel sorry for those children. They have grown up under the cruelest king to ever live. They take pleasure in their kills. They keep their swords sharp on the lesser fae and those who have renounced the winter court."

"The people who live here," I said. "So why are we here?" I looked around. "It's not for the amazing atmosphere."

He gave me the most dazzling smile. "I have a proposition for you."

"Dude, you need to work on your game."

A slow, sexy smile came over his face. "I don't think that's true."

I shook my head because I had no words. I didn't have to be a psychic to understand that his words were more than likely true.

"When the king's army is bored," Evander said, "they come

here. In small groups they go off to do their worst. Which is perfect for me."

"Them wreaking havoc is perfect?"

"My soldiers are great, but we are outnumbered ten to one. If we stormed the winter court, all the people who I call friends would die. It would be a suicide mission, and we would accomplish nothing but leaving those stuck here without protection. When the king's army comes here in small groups, we can pick them off and the king assumes that either his men bit off more than they can chew or they tried to escape. As long as we kill a few here and there it raises no brows. The king has been noted in saying that if his men can't survive in the slums, he doesn't want them in his army."

He took a swig from whatever brown, sluggish stuff was in his mug, and I winced for him. My powers swiftly reached out to see what he was thinking. I only got fragments. Jumbled pieces and words. I frowned. The key? Lost. Hunt. Human world. Time to strike.

He gave me a knowing look. "Did you find what you were looking for?"

Did he know I had the key? Of course he knew. That first night I was in his cabin he probably checked my bag. If I did that swirly black disappearing thing, I bet I could be in Cancún, Mexico in a second. Wait! The cat. I needed to grab my demon. Maybe I should swing by the cells first and grab the ol' ball and chain.

"Relax, Jolene. I have no interest in the key."

But he had answered my question. He knew that I had it.

"The first step to defeating the king was messing up his supply and demand. If he didn't have the key…"

"He could make no more soldiers." Putting Mexico on the back burner, I asked, "Did you steal the key from him?"

"In a roundabout way. Demons were sent to portal eighteen. They were to gather more children. Somehow the witches found out about the key that the demons carried and stole it from them. My soldier who was tracking the demons lost it until she went back to the hotel the witches were staying at. She saw the key in the hands of a crazy chick."

Vanka. Vanka was his soldier.

"The king doesn't know what happened to his demons. He doesn't know about the witches. He has a good portion of his men in the human world looking for the key. This is the best time to take out a few of his army while he is distracted."

"Oh, you tricky, sneaky son of an evil man. Why would you let the…" I leaned in closer. "The key anywhere near the court again?"

"It's literally the last place he would look." He was grinning as he took a sip from his glass. "Tonight we are going to have a crash course on your training. You are going to give me intel. Where the king's men are. How many there are. What their powers are. And you are going to do it all without bleeding or tiring out."

I rolled my eyes. He was asking for a lot.

"Think of it as hunting. While we're out I want you to reach for your powers. Gather them to you and practice."

"Aww," I said as I reached across the table and laid a hand over his. "This is our first date." It was meant to be funny, but when he flipped his hand so our palms were touching, a zing went up my arm.

"Do you know what they say about couples that hunt and gather together?" he asked.

"Um…they don't starve?"

He laughed before he released my hand. Then he drank whatever liquid was in the mug before pushing mine toward me. "This will help relax you. Maybe you will release your powers more easily if you're not so uptight."

Pfft. I wasn't uptight. I took a tiny sip of the murky liquid and gagged. "What is this?"

"Devil's breath."

"Oh, well that explains it." I took another giant swallow and pushed the rest away. "That's all I can do without adding to the sticky substance that is literally coating everything in here. Speaking of…" I peeled my hand away from the table. "Is there a bathroom?"

He stood up and pulled me to my feet. With one hand on my

back, he escorted me through a narrow hallway and to a door. "I'll wash up too."

"Good, because your elbows probably have contracted something by now."

He was laughing as I went into the bathroom to wash my hands. I looked at myself in the cracked and dirty mirror. The vision came swiftly, but I was prepared for it this time. I let my powers reach out and embrace the future. My hands stilled under the running faucet as images filtered to me.

CHAPTER 16

When I came out of the bathroom, Evander took one look at my face and knew something was wrong. It wasn't until he had ushered me out of the bar that he began to question me.

"Did you have a vision?"

I nodded but didn't say anything as he helped me onto his horse.

"Was it bad?"

"Very," I answered as he settled in behind me.

"Can you tell me about it?"

How did you tell someone that you had a vision of yourself falling to your knees in agony? Not because you were wounded but because someone had broken your heart. The vision of me crashing to the ground, my palms hitting the cement floor saturated with someone's blood. The blood that I'd rocked back and forth in. I didn't see whose blood, but the sounds that had been released from me were guttural. The kinds of sounds that you only make when someone extremely close to you dies.

"I can't talk about it," I said as we made our way through the village.

The truth behind that was I couldn't talk about it because I didn't know if that vision was from the future, something that I could change with more information, or my worst fear: What if it was from the past? Something that I had forgotten. When Evander healed me, I would recall that night, and could I live through it twice?

He rested his chin on top of my head. "Okay, little lamb, even though I can feel your pain, I won't push you. Take your mind off your troubles until you are ready to share them. Embrace your power and tell us where I should steer Thanatos."

Completely surrounded by him, I closed my eyes and smiled. The man was pushing his healing power into me right now, and yet he had a horse named Thanatos. The Greek word for death. I let my powers flow through me, and I realized the more I did this, the more natural it felt.

I cleared my throat. "There are two fae, one male and one female, two streets over to the right. They have decided that they want a house that belongs to the mostly humans. The family didn't inherit enough of the fae genes from their ancestors, and they won't be able to fight the fae couple off. The dad will try, and he will lose his life in front of his children. The youngest boy will make a rush for the female fae, and she will kill him."

His hands tightened around me as he steered Thanatos to the right and over two streets. He hopped from the horse and helped me down. After securing Thanatos to a potted plant that had died long ago, he took my hand, and we began going down the dirty alley on foot. I tugged on his hand, a silent command to stop.

He pulled me into the shadows between two buildings, and we waited there until a couple came walking down the alley. They stopped in front of a yellow house with peeling paint and several patches of missing shingles. The house connected to two others that were in similar shape. I didn't know why they chose this house until the female spoke up.

"Are you sure this is the house?" she asked.

"Yes," the male answered. "The mother is sick. They will be easy to overtake."

"Are we killing them?"

The man shrugged. "Up to you."

She gave him a wicked smile.

Evander dropped my hand and stepped from the shadows.

"Nice night for a stroll, isn't it?" he said with a malicious grin.

The male seemed to know Evander. He reached out to snag the female's elbow, as if to warn her off.

She jerked away. Nose in the air, she snarled, "This is our house now. We're stronger fae than the ones occupying it, so we can take it. You're not our king."

She pulled a dagger from behind her and threw it. I moved in wisps and shadows, placing myself in front of Evander. I caught the blade by the handle. The point was less than an inch away from penetrating my heart.

"Little lamb, you grow more fascinating by the second." His gaze was looking over me as if he'd just peeled back another layer.

I nodded, staring at the blade in my hand. How had that happened?

While I was preoccupied with my awesomeness, the woman attacked Evander. Me personally? If I had thrown a blade at someone and they disappeared only to reappear and catch the blade like the badass that they were, I would have run. Well first I would have dipped my head, thrown up some deuces, mumbled an apology, and run, but not this lady. She attacked with everything she had, and they called *me* crazy.

Evander stood there with his legs braced apart. When the fae woman went to strike him, he dodged her blow, never taking his eyes from the fae male circling him. I threw my hands up with frustration. Somehow Evander saw the motion.

"What's wrong, little lamb?"

"Literally disappeared and caught a knife, and they aren't even concerned about me?"

He chuckled as he dodged another attack from the female fae.

"Do you hear that?" he asked the couple. "You've hurt my lamb's feelings. I was going to kill you quickly, but now I think it will be slow."

I winked at him before I realized his back was now to me. I didn't care. The universe knew I was awkward. I shifted from foot to foot as Evander played with his prey.

My power snagged onto another vision as he simultaneously

dislocated the woman's jaw and broke the man's arm. Even at that, they still kept trying their hardest to kill him. At least they weren't quitters.

"Hate to speed this along," I said, "but we have a group of men that are about to do some sickening things." I put a hand over my queasy stomach. "Things I wish to heavens that I wouldn't have just seen. You're going to end this quicker than you had originally intended."

And just like that, the couple was dead. He snapped both of their necks and left them where they lay.

"What about the children who live in that house?"

He gave me a questioning look. "Do we have time?"

"We have an hour, but we need to get into a good position."

He grabbed the bodies and threw them in a big box that looked like a dumpster. Then he went up the steps to the yellow house.

"Where are you going?" I hissed.

"You said we had an hour, correct?"

I nodded.

"Then we have time to heal the mom. Come on. I can't leave you in the street."

Again I was speechless. Not that I remembered any of my first dates, but even if I had, this would have been the best first date ever. After healing the mother, Evander awkwardly patted the kids' heads. He shook the husband's hand. The man had tears in his eyes as Evander told them to contact him if they ever needed anything.

After we left their home, Evander showed me nothing but patience as he taught me how to call the visions to me. We were some pair. I gathered. He hunted. We did this until the sun was starting to peak over the mountains. After returning to the cabin and a sleeping demon, he took me to his room. He pulled the covers over me and then climbed on top of the blankets where we spooned together. As his healing powers poured into me, I realized he hadn't asked me again about the Winter King's army.

"Evander?"

"Hmm."

"Ten thousand strong," I mumbled sleepily.

I felt his body tense, then he relaxed once again. "Go to sleep, little lamb."

Cocooned in his arms, I rested as his power mingled with mine, bringing me peace.

CHAPTER 17

A throat was clearing. I opened one eye to see the cat on the end of the bed. There was a golden arm draped over me. With a smile on my lips, I closed my eyes and snuggled deeper into the mattress. The voice cleared again, and this time it was louder. Evander threw a pillow at the cat and missed.

The demon snickered. "Look at you two, all snuggly. I sure do hope your mate is a chill fellow."

Lifting the heavy arm from me, I sat up in bed. Crap. I had forgotten about um…Calvin?

I turned to see Evander lying in bed with one arm over his eyes and a giant smile on his face.

"Why is he smiling?" my cat asked.

"Yeah, why are you smiling?"

Evander dropped his arm, his warm, golden eyes meeting mine. "How do you feel?"

"Great. I had more memories come back to me and everything is starting to fall back into place."

He nodded. "What's the demon's name?"

"Fatimah."

"Do you remember everything about last night?"

What a crazy question. Of course I remembered everything about last night.

"Yes, I gathered, you hunted. The streets ran red with the blood of bad men. We were a dynamic duo."

He gave me a small smile. "True. What's your mate's name again?"

I pointed at my demon who knew exactly what I was requiring of him and supplied the missing info. "Calhoun," he said with a flick of his tail.

Evander stretched his arms above his head, his muscles stretching and making my mouth water. Why was he so hot? I swung my legs over the bed and stood, just to make sure I didn't do anything crazy like throw myself at him.

"Don't you think if Calhoun was your mate, you would remember his name?"

I put my hands on my hips. "I once was in love with a man who couldn't remember what I looked like. He searched over the whole kingdom for me and the only description he had was a size seven glass slipper that I had accidentally left behind. He literally tried the shoe on every girl in the kingdom to see if it fit."

Fatimah groaned. "Again, that was a movie. However, I would just like everyone in this room to know that I have never sat down to watch something so mundane."

I winced. "So most of my memories are coming back and some things I'm uncertain if it happened to me or someone else. Good news is I can remember my friends. My childhood. My sweet granny. Technically she's my best friend's grandmother, but she raised me, so it's like she's mine too."

"I think his point is," the cat said, "you should probably make a better effort of remembering Calhoun's name."

I snapped my finger. "I'll write it down."

Evander stood slowly. "You might want to write down his description as well."

I shouted at his retreating back. "I don't know why that bugs you so bad."

He was mumbling something as he went into the bathroom.

"Oh I hope he comes out in a towel again," Fatimah begged.

I sat on the edge of the bed as I felt a vision coming. My powers stretched out as I embraced it. This time I zeroed in on what I wanted to see more of and fast-forwarded through the parts I deemed insignificant. I was still sitting there when Evander came out of the bathroom—much to Fatimah's horror—fully dressed for the day.

He stood directly in front of me. With one finger, he tilted up my chin. "You want to tell me about this one?"

I sighed. "No, but I should. Some of the beings trained by the king are rambunctious. The king has control over them with the collars, but he no longer wants them right under his nose. He is planning on clearing out the slums of their inhabitants and then allowing the difficult factions to live here until he has use of them."

"When?"

"They come tomorrow."

"Then we need to leave," the demon said.

I was shocked to see Evander agreeing. "Yes, you should head out now."

"I'm not leaving."

Both the cat and Evander looked at me like I was being unreasonable. "Listen," I said, "I'm here because this is exactly where I'm supposed to be. I'm not going anywhere."

"So you are willing to die alongside me and my soldiers tomorrow?"

I waved a hand. "Oh I might have left out some details. Sorry. You don't die tomorrow. You win the battle, but when you kill fifteen percent—roughly fifteen hundred men—from the king's army, he is going to want to do some investigative work. That research will lead to a battle that is like nothing history has ever seen." What I failed to mention was the guard that he was debating whether to kill or not escaped last night—with my help, of course. I woke in the middle of the night, did my disappearing act, and let him out. I was returned to Evander's arms in less than three minutes. I went back to bed in awe of myself. Totally badass.

Timelines. I had to keep everyone on the right timeline.

"And do we win that battle?"

I shrugged. "Didn't see that, but I got to be honest with you, it doesn't look good." I sighed heavily. "I'm super sad."

His hand reached out and lightly cupped my jaw, his thumb gently caressing my cheek. "Why's that, little lamb?"

"Your power is like no other. It's even more powerful than the king's. He wants to break your mind. Find out who you are and why you are here in No Man's Land. He wants to know everything about you." I wet my lips, and his golden eyes tracked the motion. "There's one issue with that."

"What?" he whispered.

"They shouldn't be able to bring you in alive. You willingly go with them." I shook my head. "It doesn't make sense. Without you, these people...your soldiers don't have a chance to win the coming battle, so why would you go with them?"

He dropped his hand to his side. "The only thing I can think of is that they took something from me that made me feel like the battle was no longer worth fighting."

I scrunched up my face. I didn't know Evander exceptionally well, but that didn't sound like him at all. He didn't give up. He didn't have the air about him that he was a quitter.

The cat groaned. "Great. We're staying to fight a battle that is already doomed." He hopped from the bed and started walking to the door. "I'm going to go see if there is an unlimited supply of sequins."

"Why?" I asked.

"Duh, so I can alter the soldiers' outfits. Just because we're all going to die doesn't mean that we shouldn't look fabulous with our last breaths."

As soon as he was out the door, Evander said, "If he touches my soldiers' gear, I'll kill him."

"I would expect no less."

He ran a hand through his black hair. "Get dressed, little lamb. We are going to try to gather all the non-fae and get them out of this realm. That's if they want to go. If they want to stay and fight, I'll let them."

I frowned. "They will just get in the way, or worse, get killed."

"There are worse things than dying. Some of these men who live here in the slums, whether they are fae or human, are proud men. They have had nothing but their name and their home. If they want to defend their land, I'll not get in the way." He walked to the door. "Get dressed and meet me outside. We have a lot to do today."

I quickly threw on some clothes he had put in a drawer for me and followed him outside. Evander was healing me with every touch, and I was starting to become more grounded. His power was pouring into me, and in return my power hummed. We were riding through one of the villages when a vision came to me. More like a memory. A memory of the past. Tears were streaming down my face as we passed a field with nothing but dirt and clay mounds.

His voice was just a whisper. "Little lamb? What is it?"

How could I tell him about this last memory? How could I voice my embarrassment, hurt, and grief out loud? For the first time, I regretted Evander healing me.

CHAPTER 18

His hands tightened around me, and his chin rested on the top of my head. "I can feel your grief. How can I fix this?"

"You can't." I hiccupped. "I'll give you the information you need regarding the sentry headed your way, and then I need to go."

His arms flexed around my waist before they relaxed a smidge. "Where are you going, Jolene?"

I shrugged, another hiccup escaping my body. "I don't know. I don't care."

He was quiet as we continued down the road, passing a few early risers. He took a side road with broken-up cobblestones. The houses were connected to one another, and smoke was coming out of more chimneys than not. I was lost in my own thoughts as he exited out of the village and into the surrounding forest. He was pumping his healing energy into me. I could feel it and I hated it.

I tried to pull away, but his arms tightened.

"Don't heal me, please." The last word was more of a whispered plea.

I needed to go. To run, but to where? It didn't matter. I just needed to get away from Evander. I couldn't let him heal me anymore. As if sensing where my mind was, he swung from the horse and all but jerked me from the saddle. His hand was holding onto my wrist with enough force that it broke through my dark thoughts.

"You are many things, little lamb, but you are not a coward. If you run, I will find you, and whatever you are hiding from, I'll force you to face."

Tears were streaming down my cheeks. "Why? How could you be so cruel?"

He bent his knees so his eyes were level with mine. "I'm a badass, remember? We don't care who we offend. It's not my job to worry about others' perception of my moral code, not when protecting you from burnout is more important than protecting your feelings. If you leave here, you will burn out. Not because you have mastered how to control your powers—that I could almost live with—but because you are choosing the cowardly way out. You are choosing to forget who you are. I want to know why."

I opened my mouth but closed it again. How do I begin? Once I said it out loud, there would be no taking it back.

"Talk to me, little lamb, and I'll make you a deal. If you still want to run, I'll let you."

"What if I tell you, and then you demand I leave?"

His jaw clenched and slowly straightened his legs so that he towered over me. "I wouldn't do that to you."

I scoffed. "From what I have seen, you have bigger problems headed your way than my burnout, unless you think that I have more information I can give to you." I shook my head fiercely. "Which I don't."

"I'm worried about you. Not the future. Do we have a deal?"

I nodded and he released my wrist. "Ariana had been working with me. Teaching me how to embrace my powers. I was overworked and tired, and some days I slipped between teetering on the edge of a burnout and being lucid. My friends…all their timelines were intersecting and crisscrossing, and I was trying so hard to keep everything straight. Considering I had the past, present, and future flashing to me along with every road they could possibly take, and which road would be the best for them, their kingdom, and our future as a whole, I think I was doing a good job."

Evander gave me an encouraging nod when I hesitated.

"I messed up, though. I saw something happening to a loved one. Something that I could have prevented." My hands raised a little and then flopped back down to my sides. "I let someone I love die."

"Walk me through it," he said.

"I don't want to."

"You had once admired my soldiers. Do you remember that?"

I bit my lip and gave him a small nod even though I couldn't make eye contact.

"They became what they are today not because they don't harbor fear, but because they push through whatever obstacles are in their way. Today we will ask them to fight against a group of demons coming our way. I will be honest and let them know what you have witnessed. This doesn't mean that we will win the war. In fact, there's a slim chance that all our lives will get substantially worse when we win this battle." He put a finger under my chin and forced me to look at him. "Did you see them fighting in the last battle?"

"Yes."

"Do you know what that means? They know they will die, but they will still choose to go down on their own terms. Of course they are going to be afraid, but they will use that fear to take as many of the Winter King's army down with them as they can. You can run from your memories, little lamb, or you can lock your legs, spread your arms out wide, tilt your chin up, and you can own it. Your choice."

Grief poured over me again. Regaining my memories was as if I was enduring the pain all over again. There was only one way to retell what I had done, and that was to hurry through it.

"Seven keys. There are seven keys to fifty-nine portals. It is important that the right people have the keys. If the wrong people—like the Winter King—have them, then, well you see what he has done. What he is capable of doing."

Evander dropped his hand from my chin and nodded. "Go on."

"I was orchestrating getting the right keys to the right people. Ariana has wanted to retire for centuries, but she hasn't found someone to take her place until me." I scoffed. "Obviously she chose wrong." I shifted my feet on the dirt path. "I witnessed my granny dying. The woman who raised me. My best friend's real grandmother." Tears rolled down my face. "She gave me a home when I didn't have one. She protected me like I was hers. When my powers were consuming me, she would drop in just to bring me food. She was so worried I'd forget to eat. She thought my job was the most important job in the world, and she thought it was her job to keep me functioning. I witnessed a human robbing her. Not a demon, a shifter, or any other faction that could have easily taken her down, but a scrawny human who wasn't even of drinking age yet. I knew the time, the place—I had all the information to save her life."

My knees felt as if they were going to give out on me. I closed my eyes and took several deep breaths. "When the vision came to me, I was in the middle of saving a pregnant woman. She was no one to me. But her child will grow up to be someone very powerful, and he will help keep the balance between good and evil. She was in the wrong place and the wrong time." I laughed without any trace of humor. "I hate it when people say that. No, she was right where she was supposed to be. A shifter was about to kill her because she had refused him as her mate. She had found someone else who was more honorable and was her true mate. The shifter that was after her was ruled by jealousy, and he was going to kill the mother and the child. Since I was already there, I thought I could save the mother and unborn child, and then I'd have time to rescue my grandmother. Time to get back to the one person who has ever loved me unconditionally."

I lifted my gaze to meet his eyes. "I didn't foresee that I would be wounded saving the mother." My mouth opened and closed as I tried to find the words to describe the horror I felt when I realized that I wasn't going to make it on time to save my granny. "I can heal super fast. Did you know that?"

"I didn't know that, little lamb." He shook his head, and his voice was so low, as if he was scared to spook me.

"I can. It wasn't fast enough, though. When I arrived in the parking lot, my granny was lying on the pavement. She died in a grocery store parking lot because I didn't choose her." My body was shaking. "Do you know what she said with her last breath?"

He shook his head.

"She said, 'Do not beat yourself up over this.' Her last concern was over someone who could have saved her and failed to do so."

Strong arms came around me as my body shook with sobs. He was mumbling soft words, but I couldn't hear them, not over the guttural sounds I was making.

I don't know how long we stood there, but when I had finally calmed down, the sun was high in the sky and the morning dew had disappeared from the leaves.

Evander pulled back so he could look at me, but he kept his arms around me, and for that I was grateful. I felt so alone.

"I want to tell you something. I want you to listen, but it's up to you if you believe me or not."

"Okay," I said on a shaky breath.

"You were saving a mother and a child. Never feel bad about that. Did you have any visions about your grandmother passing before you went to save this mother and child?"

I shook my head. "No, it was in the middle of trapping the psychotic shifter when the vision of my granny came to me. I knew by the bank clock next to the grocery store that I had thirty minutes to get to her. As soon as the vision cleared, the shifter swiped at me, almost spilling my guts onto the floor of the mother's house. It took me a little longer to end him, and then I was weak, which made traveling to her longer than anticipated."

He put both of his hands on my cheeks. "What happened then?"

"I tried to call my best friend. I couldn't get a hold of her. I knew she would never reach her in time. I could only travel in small blips. Gain my strength and travel again. In between, I kept trying to call my granny." A half-smile lit my face. "She never liked taking her cell phone. I called the store, but no one would pick up the phone. I was listening to an advertisement about rib eyes as I finally landed in the parking lot."

"You did everything you could to warn your grandmother, and you—"

I shook my head. "No, I could have left right away. I could have chosen her."

He cocked his head to the side. "Could you have though?"

"Of course I could have."

"But you said that the vision came while you were fighting the shifter, correct?"

"Yes, but—"

"You were distracted with the new vision…the one of your grandmother dying and you got wounded, correct?"

"Yes…"

Evander gave me a tender smile. "And then when you were wounded, you couldn't travel as fast, correct?"

Reluctantly I nodded.

"Jolene, there was nothing you could have done to alter your grandmother's future. You did not kill her."

"I could've—"

"There was nothing you could have done. If you want me to track down the human and rip his entrails from his body and let him die in agony before you, I will. I'll present him like a feast before a queen. If you want me to hold you while you properly grieve for the loss of a loved one, I will. But if you want me to believe that you are responsible for her death because you feel guilty over something that you should bear no guilt for, then that's where I have to disagree."

He pulled my face to his chest and held me in the most tender hold I've ever felt. I gripped the sides of his shirt and, for the first time in a long time, I took deep, calming breaths as I inhaled his scent.

Who would have thought that the scary man holding me was capable of such tenderness? I took another deep breath. Everything was going to be okay. The sun would keep rising. The world would keep turning, and for the first time I truly felt like maybe I had a chance. Maybe I wouldn't burn out. I owed a lot of my feelings of gratitude to Evander. Without him, I think I would be lying in a cot somewhere just like Madeline. Craving peace through any means.

I mumbled into his shirt. "My granny would have been obsessed with you."

He stroked my back. "And why is that, little lamb?"

Oh he knew why. He was sexy and even more devilishly handsome when he smirked. He made lady bits warm just by walking into a room. Even my demon was obsessed. He was a man who knew what he wanted and how to get it. I had received a lot more from Evander than I had given. More peace surrounded my life just because he was in it. He was a man worth obsessing over.

"Maybe she liked villains."

He laughed as he led me back to his horse. "And I have a feeling that she would be very proud of you."

His words rang true. My heart lightened, and I felt the cracks in me being mended.

"Let's go prepare my soldiers. We will talk with them, and then after, I promise you can rest."

Once I was back on the horse, I snuggled into him as he continued to pour his power into me. I would heal. I would still grieve for the woman I lost, but I would heal. Then I would seek out my best friend and make her understand that what happened to Granny wasn't something that I could stop. Much like the war that would be upon us. Some things—no matter how hard you tried to stop or manipulate—just wouldn't budge.

CHAPTER 19

EVANDER HAD ROUNDED UP ALL HIS MEN AND WOMEN INTO A dilapidated warehouse that served as both their training center and storage space for their supplies. He had enough to fuel an army three times as big as the one he commanded. I stood next to him as he addressed the three hundred soldiers.

He had given them two options. Either stay and fight the upcoming battle and know that winning meant war on the horizon. A war that they may not win. Or they could leave the fae world. Gather their family today and disappear before the battle began. I personally thought that he wasn't really selling the whole 'we need help so stay and fight' bit, so I was surprised when they all stayed. Their stance seemed to widen, and their chins were thrust in the air as Evander nodded at them in gratitude.

He cleared his throat. "Jolene will tell us what she saw and what to expect."

I gave him my best 'are you kidding me' look. I didn't do public speaking. I plastered on a too-wide grin and gave a little wave to the stony-faced warriors. "So, um…hi. As some of you may know, I see things, past, present, and future. I had a vision of a battle that will happen as soon as the sun goes down. The Winter King will send over his degenerates, the ones who don't fit in and are crowding his court with their ill manners and monstrosities. There are two ways that this can go down. We can attack as they are crossing the bridge. You'll be without a bridge, but there will be zero casualties. Or you wait until they meet you in the first village and there will be several casualties."

A man with a short buzz cut looked to each side of him before addressing me. "If there are zero casualties in the first option, then we will go with it."

A man behind him laughed. "Yeah, zero is a number I can live with."

"Killing them on the bridge means that you knew they were coming. The Winter King will find out about me. He'll be intrigued, and instead of just squashing us all in the final war, he will try to find me." I cleared my throat. "So, from what I'm seeing, the end result will either be quick and almost painless, or long and drawn out in a ferocious battle with lots of pain." The soldiers shifted on their feet. I frowned. Maybe I was making their morale go down. "My point is that even though you will more than likely lose, you all will go down as legends. This will be an epic tale of sacrifice and heroism…mostly sacrifice, though."

Vanka who was in the second row laughed. "Dang. Maybe we shouldn't put you in charge of our pep talks."

I looked over at Evander, who was pinching the bridge of his nose. I threw my hands up.

Evander dropped his hand and sighed. "Jolene, how about you tell them why you are uncertain if they will lose or not."

I hid my smile. "I swear I was getting to that." I winked at the wide-eyed men and women. "There are things that can manipulate the future. I have foreseen the upcoming war with plenty of time to brainstorm something we can do to change the outcome."

The man with a buzz cut nodded. "So there's a chance that we all won't die?"

Small. Minimal. Really barely there. "Yes!"

Someone clapped buzzcut on the back, and the crowd seemed to settle a little.

Evander spoke loud and clear. "We ready the bridge. We take down as many of them as we can before they step foot in No Man's Land. The others we stop before they get to the village."

Evander dismissed everyone to go prepare for battle, and I

stood off to the side, waiting for the last stragglers to exit. When the last one was gone, Evander strolled over to me with a smile on his face.

Immediately I was suspicious, especially after the announcement that I had just butchered.

"I need you to go to the cabin and relax."

"Why?"

"You might just be our saving grace."

Definitely suspicious now. "How so?"

"If you practice with your gift, you might be able to figure out a way for us to win this war."

I shook my head in dismay as Evander escorted me back to his cabin. I had seen three different outcomes for the upcoming war. I didn't dare voice the third option, because that would mean that I would have to put on my big girl panties and face my fears. I'd have to seek out my best friend and ask her for forgiveness, and then I'd have to ask her for help. Along with others who hold the keys. I didn't know if I could do that, but I also didn't know if I could allow Evander, along with everyone here in No Man's Land, to be slaughtered.

CHAPTER 20

FATIMAH FLICKED HIS TAIL NEXT TO A FLOWER THAT WAS TRYING TO eat him for lunch. Every few seconds he would snicker.

I stood on the hill with a few of the soldiers.

"I'm going to laugh when that plant eats you," Vanka said as she came to stand next to me.

The cat arched his tail over the flower's jaws. "I'm too fast for you, boyo."

"You really shouldn't play with the flowers," I said to Fatimah before asking Vanka, "Evander will be the only one fighting on the bridge?"

"Yes," Vanka replied. "After he is done, we will go down and retrieve heads and hearts."

I opened my powers several times today to make sure that my earlier vision was right. The truth was Evander didn't need any help. He was actually saving a few from getting hurt, but there was something inside of me that didn't like that he was down there all alone.

The cat hissed as he jumped a foot in the air. "Bad flower. Bad flower!" He came to stand in between me and Vanka. "The plant took part of my fur off. I'm not playing with him anymore."

Vanka was giving my cat a funny look. "He's strange."

I snorted. "Who isn't?"

Before she could say anything else, we saw the demon army

crossing the first bridge into No Man's Land. Evander stood on the other side, both hands clasped behind his back. His muscles were tense and ready for the upcoming battle.

"Where is his sword?" Fathima asked.

"He won't need it," I replied.

"I'm going to need some clarification," the cat said.

Vanka laughed. "You are in for a treat today." She walked off when another soldier waved her over.

"What's that supposed to mean?" Fathima asked.

I squatted down so I was closer to the cat but could still see Evander. "It means that Evander is the most powerful fae to ever live. He shouldn't exist, and yet he does."

Fathima stared at me for a few seconds before turning his stare to Evander. "Okay, I'll buy that, but if he is so powerful, why can't he defeat the Winter King's whole army?"

"We are talking about ten thousand beings, Fatty. It's impossible."

Not impossible. I could ask my friends and that would help our cause, but even then I wasn't seeing a clear victory. Earlier I had almost warmed up to the idea of asking them, but the more I thought about it the less I liked it. What if I asked them and they ended up dying? Or their mates? I rubbed my forehead. How much more loss could I take? What if I broke again?

My eyes jerked to the bridge in preparation. Even knowing what was coming, I still flinched as the bridge blew up. Out of two hundred and fifty men there were now a hundred or so left. The ones that were still lucky enough to be alive were trying to figure a way up the small embankment. As they were scrambling, I watched the plants, trees, and water under the bridge come to life.

Vines seemed to fall out of trees as they sprung out and lashed around the demons' necks like whips. The nooses tightened, and I turned my head as unmistakable pops went off at different times.

"Well," Fatimah said, "that's a new way of beheading someone."

The river water rose and formed iced swords that spiraled toward the demons. Flowers sprung from the ground and towered over any demons that had made it up the embankment. The petals seemed to pull back moments before they ate the demons whole.

Fatimah scooted closer to me. "Okay, I'm officially freaked out."

"I told you not to play with the flowers."

"Maybe be a little more specific next time," he grumbled. "If I would have known that they can grow to the size of giraffes, I probably would've been a little more chill and kept my distance."

"Shh," I said. "This is my favorite part."

The sun seemed to beam down on Evander as he stood there with his hands still clasped behind his back. Five demons charged him, and a bright light emitted from him. The demons were left as nothing but ash. Somehow he had fried them.

"Um…ah…" Fatimah said. "So I have questions. Mainly what the hell just happened?"

"He just killed the approaching demons."

"Yeah, I got that. I mean barely. I blinked and then the demons were just ashes blowing in the wind, so I'm still not certain that I'm not hallucinating."

"You're not seeing things," I said while the plants devoured the remaining demons. "He can kill without touching. Remember how he told you that?"

"Yeah," Fatimah said nervously, "but I guess I didn't realize he was *that* powerful."

"The energy that he uses takes a lot out of him. He can do it once in about a twenty-four-hour period. Also, he has to be within so many feet before he releases it."

The cat nodded. "Good to know."

I couldn't pass up this opportunity to mess with my demon, so I said, "But the cabin is small."

His dark eyes darted over to me. "Yeah, but he wouldn't waste that burst of power on little ol' me, right?"

When I didn't say anything, he repeated, "Right?"

Hiding my smile, I shrugged as the soldiers started heading down the hill. I sighed. "Show's over."

When Evander turned and started making his way up the hill,

Fatimah coughed and excused himself. My cat was officially terrified of the handsome fae.

Halfway up the hill, Evander intercepted Shay. "Put their heads on spikes. If we are going to send a message, we might as well send a message."

I almost fainted right then and there. That had to be the sexiest thing I had ever heard. His eyes flitted over to mine as if he could hear my thoughts. A smirk crossed his face as he continued to walk toward me.

"Was it the 'head on spikes' remark?"

He knew that I was about to have to hose myself down. Why lie? I nodded. "Call me crazy, most do, but there's something very erotic about a man willing to make a statement."

With a grin on his face, he shook his head. "Come with me, little lamb."

He held out his hand, and I took it without hesitation. "Where are we going?"

His power was pumping into me. All the little cracks were healing. Not only were they healing, but I felt better than I did even before I broke.

"We have a lot to do before the Winter King comes." We were walking silently back to his horse. After he helped me on then climbed behind me, he said, "I have a lot of questions I would like for you to answer, and then I want you to leave tonight."

I half turned in the saddle. "Leave?"

His jaw was tense. "It's not up for discussion."

I turned forward and lifted my shoulders. "You can't make me."

"Yes, I can."

"What are you going to do? Fry me like you did the demons? I happen to know those little bursts of energy take a while to build back up. If you want to kill me without touching me, you'll have to wait until tomorrow." I leaned back into his arms and yawned.

He shifted his arms so they were tighter around me. "You do realize that I can kill by touching, too, right?"

I closed my eyes and smiled. There were worse ways to die than a hot fae male touching you to death.

"What am I going to do with you, little lamb?"

Sleepily I answered, "I don't know, but sending me home isn't an option. I'm going to see this through."

His voice was tight with emotion. "You are human. You will die."

"I'm going to be honest with you, I really never thought I'd make it this far."

He was quiet for a few moments. There were no sounds other than the hooves beating on the ground as we made haste toward his cabin.

Finally, he said, "I don't like how flippant you are about your life ending."

I snuggled deeper into his arms. "I'd say I'd work on that, but you would hear the lie."

He half growled, causing me to smile. Neither of us spoke again until we reached the cabin. When he helped me from the horse, his hands stayed on my waist a little longer than normal. His eyes darted to my lips and then to my eyes. There was no masking the desire that burned in them. I didn't blink. I couldn't tear my gaze away from his handsome face. He leaned forward, and then his brows creased. I didn't mean to listen to his thoughts, but I was trying to understand the hesitation.

"Can't give her a reason to stay."

His eyes flicked to mine. He knew that I had heard him.

My arms wrapped around his neck. "I already told you that I'm staying. Might as well make it worth my while."

Then I tugged his face lower. The moment his lips touched mine, my whole body felt like I was on fire. His breathing came deeper when I let out a tiny moan. My hips rocked into his when his fingers tightened on the small of my back. Something in my belly unraveled as a sensation that I had never felt before rippled through me like tiny little tremors. His tongue met mine like he was claiming me. Marking me as his. How could a kiss bring so much pleasure?

I pulled back from him with a frown on my face.

He swiped my bottom lip with his thumb. "That wasn't quite the reaction I was hoping for, and need I remind you that *you* kissed *me*?"

I played with the hair at the back of his nape for a few precious seconds before I dropped my hands and stepped away.

His brows crashed together. "What's wrong, little lamb?"

What was wrong? Oh, there was a list. When I kissed him, my power opened up. No, that's too generic of a word. It freaking *bloomed*. It was currently humming through my body like a live wire. My fingers went to my swollen lips. And I was a cheater. Oh, poor Cadence. Caden? Camden? Oh shit. I closed my eyes and hit my palm to my forehead. I was a horrible, horrible human.

Gentle fingers pressed under my chin, forcing me to look up. "What's wrong?"

"Um…I probably shouldn't have kissed you."

His eyes twinkled. "Yeah, but I thoroughly enjoyed it, and how do you know if something is a mistake if you don't do it more than once?"

I rolled my eyes. "You forget, dear sir, that I am practically a married woman."

His lips twitched. "Yeah, and what's your mate's name again?" When I just narrowed my eyes at him, he tilted his head back and laughed. "You know, for someone that claims to have found her true mate, you sure do struggle with his name."

Because he had a point and I really hated admitting defeat, I turned on my heel and started walking to the cabin. His next words stopped me.

"Eyes that are blue, but when the sun hits just right they turn to a light green. Skin so flawless that even the high fae would be jealous. Full lips that are the color of raspberries. When you are thinking about something sad, you bite your bottom lip and your brows come together. When you are thinking of something funny, one side of your mouth raises higher than the other. Though your beauty is beyond compare, your heart might just be your most endearing quality. Anyone who can love like you fears disappointing others. And to take in a stray demon requires a huge heart."

He was talking about me. Without turning around, I said, "Or I could be crazy." When he didn't say anything, I turned. "What are you doing right now?"

He was proving a point. "You couldn't remember Calhoun's eye color."

He walked toward me, and I couldn't tear my gaze away from his beautiful features. He leaned down and gently kissed me on my forehead. "I want you to go somewhere safe, but if you refuse to go, then you leave me no choice."

When he walked past me, I said, "Wait! What do you mean?"

He whistled as he walked into the cabin. "Aren't you supposed to be a psychic?"

At a loss for words, I trailed behind him. Before I could say anything, the cat jumped from the couch and made a wide berth around Evander. He practically hid behind me while Evander went into the bathroom.

"What are you doing?" I whispered to Fatimah.

"I keep replaying the way he just disintegrated those demons. It's no secret how that man feels about me. I don't want to be cremated."

I rolled my eyes. "Don't be silly. He's not going to barbeque you while he is trying to conserve powers."

"So, you think I could stand here and gawk when he exits the shower?"

I started walking to the bedroom. "I wouldn't push your luck. Besides, I need you to cover for me."

"What are you going to do?"

"Visit a friend really quickly."

He hissed. "Are you out of your mind?"

"Most definitely."

I closed the door behind us and ignored the cat's pleas. It was past time I visited my best friend and explained to her what happened that night. It was the least that I could do. Plus, with Evander's healing, I now had most of my memories back. I remembered all the important people in my life.

My best friend Sadie's husband, CG, was the king of werewolves. He was fair and had a good head on his shoulders. More importantly, he loved my best friend. She was a one-of-a-kind power manipulator, and we needed her here in the fae realm. There was no question about it. They could help us win this war, but they were just a small part of it.

CG's brother Jamison was an equally powerful shifter, and his wife, Charlie, was one of the most powerful witches to ever live. She was currently working on reining in her powers so—like me—she didn't burn out. Her best friend, Tandi, and Tandi's mate were vampires. The strongest in their faction.

Austin was my first crush and also Sadie's brother. He could manipulate the space around him, jumping from one spot to the next, and he had snagged the one being that was always walking a tight line between good and evil: Carmen. She was a woman who constantly fought an eternal battle. Without her mate, she would lose the fight.

Death—aka Wes, who was also Tandi's brother—was as hot as his scythe was scary. His power was like no other. Fate had the last laugh, pairing him with the Zombie Queen. She could raise the dead, and he lays the dead to rest. A conflict of interest if I'd ever seen one.

Kian was the king of the sea, and although he was deadly in the water, he was just as deadly on land. His mate, Sasha, was a warrior through and through.

We needed them to be here to fight. We needed them on our side. I've looked at all the options. Without them, humanity will not exist in six months. Eight months, tops. And that assumed they were willing to fight alongside us. I needed every single one of them, and I still didn't know if that would be enough.

CHAPTER 21

My power was still running through my veins. It had been since that kiss. I closed my eyes and imagined where I needed to go. My black shadows carried me as if I was riding a gust of wind. Within moments I was inside a rustic mansion. The four-story house made of hewn stones and hardy boards screamed shifter.

Emotions swirled around me as I let my shadows carry me toward my best friend. She sat on a chaise lounge in front of a fire. The moment she felt my presence, she stood, dropping the book she had on her. I was trying to form words to convey my guilt when she ran to me and threw her arms around me. She was sobbing as I hugged her back.

"I'm so sorry," I said.

She pulled back from me and said, "CG said your scent was all over Granny. In some idiotic way you probably blame yourself, and for that I'm so mad at you."

I sniffled. "I do…I mean I did blame myself."

She pulled me to the chaise lounge. "Tell me everything."

I started from the beginning, and by the time I was done telling her of that tragic day, we were both wracked with tears.

"Granny loved you," she said.

I jerked my head in acknowledgment.

"If she was here right now, she would be so disappointed in you."

My heart broke into a million pieces.

"Look at me," Sadie said. When my eyes drifted to her green ones, she shook her head. "How could you ever doubt our love for you?"

"What?"

"We were raised practically as sisters. Let me ask you a question. If I had your ability and I saw something horrific involving a loved one and I didn't prevent it, would you think the worst of me?"

I played with the hem of my shirt. "No, I would assume there was a reason. Maybe someone kidnapped you. Maybe you were hurt—I don't know."

Her voice shook with rage. "And yet you doubted my faith in you. Do you know that when you disappeared, I thought someone had killed you? I mean that's the only reason that my best friend would just disappear without a word to anyone."

"I'm so sorry. I…I broke."

Tears streamed down her face. "That explains a lot. I'm going to tell you something, though…no matter what happens in our future, don't ever doubt my love for you again. Okay? Some people are meant to come into our lives and exit when the timing is right, and then some people are bound to us through a deep connection. Whether it's our soulmate, soul sister, or a family member…someone like Granny. I'll always have a piece of her with me. You are my soul sister. Our connection can't be broken. Have faith in us. I know in my heart if there had been something you could have done to prevent Granny's death, you would have. Have faith in yourself and have faith in me."

"I'm sorry." I hiccupped.

She pulled me into her arms. "I'm sorry too. I shouldn't have yelled. I've just been so worried about you."

I had planned on coming, begging her forgiveness, and then seeing where that landed us. I hadn't planned on telling her of my adventures. The truth was I had underestimated my best friend. I never once thought of searching for her through my visions because I was terrified of what I'd see. She had a father, a brother, and she had the most wonderful grandmother. All I had was her family. It made me insecure. Made me doubt their love for me.

Sadie's mate came in at some point and brought us both hot tea. He didn't say a word as he put the cups down on a table, kissed Sadie on her head, and left.

"I like him," I said.

She laughed. "I like him, too." One elegant brow rose. "So you've found your mate?"

I wrinkled my nose. "Yeah, um, Camden."

"What are the odds of us having mates with the same first name?"

Slim. "Yeah, maybe that's not his name. Here's the thing, you know how I've always struggled with names and—"

"To clarify, you've always struggled with the names of people you have found uninteresting," she said.

I winced. She wasn't making this any easier on me. "Yeah, so I can't remember his name."

Her mouth rounded in shock. "You can't remember your mate's name?"

I grabbed my tea. "Yeah, it's probably just a weird coincidence."

"Have you tried to search your future?"

I looked at her in horror. "No way. I mean sometimes I get glimpses, but I try really hard not to see anything in my future. Can you imagine seeing your own death?"

She held up both hands. "I'm just saying, I don't think fate would be so cruel to pair you with a boring mate."

I put my tea on the table and sat up straighter. "I'm not here to talk about um…Carter."

She arched her brow, but she didn't say anything. Finally, she cleared her throat. "So you've predicted a war?"

"The Winter King has been forming an army of soldiers and he is ten thousand strong. It will start in the fae realm and then it will come to the human world. Evander, the fae that has been healing me, is the most powerful fae in the realm, but that's not enough. His army is strong, but they only amount to three hundred. They are incredibly outnumbered."

"There's no chance of winning with those odds. I will gather the others, and we will meet you."

"What if one of you gets hurt? I'm almost positive that one of you will be harmed, if not get killed."

She tilted her head to the side. "What if *you* get hurt? What if you die? We all knew our job wasn't done by just accepting to protect our key. We all knew what we were signing up for. If I need to round everyone up to save humanity, I promise you they won't argue."

Again I nodded. "I know you're right. Plus I have seen a vision with a more favorable outcome, but here is the thing: The visions I'm getting are conflicted. We will only win if everything is timed perfectly. With that many beings—ten thousand against maybe three hundred—there isn't a good chance that I can get everything on the correct timeline. When you go to tell the others, I need you to make it very clear that signing up for this could be them walking to their own funeral."

"So what's the alternative? We sit and wait for the army to come to this world? We either fight and die trying, or we fail humanity."

"I agree."

She reached out and grabbed my hand. "When do we need to be in the fae realm?"

"Two days from now." I closed my eyes. "Exactly thirty-six hours and fifteen minutes."

Her eyes flickered to the huge clock on the mantel. Nodding, she stood. "Then I have so much to do and very little time to do it. Come, let me get you a room."

I stood too. "I have to get back to Evander and let him know that you are gathering as many as you can."

Her lips twitched. "Oh yes, the fae whose name you can actually remember. Tell me, Jo, is he hot?"

My eyes rolled back in my head as I moaned. "You have no freaking clue how hot."

She laughed. "Oh, well, this should all be interesting."

Returning to the main subject, I said, "We have a war to win."

She tilted her head at me. "We won't lose, baby girl."

I gave her one more hug and let my shadows take me back to the little cabin in the creepy ass forest. As the shadows receded and I witnessed what was right before me, the smile died on my lips.

CHAPTER 22

EVANDER STOOD IN THE BEDROOM WITH SWEATPANTS HUNG LOW on his hips, but that wasn't the shocking part. He had Fatimah by the neck and was shaking my poor cat. I swatted Evander on the shoulder several times.

"Put my kitty down, you meany!"

He dropped the cat and glared at me. "Where have you been?"

"Um…visiting a friend." My eyes narrowed. "Wait, didn't you tell me that you wanted me to go?"

"Yeah, but…" He ran a hand down his face while Fatimah made a break for it and ran out of the room. "I thought you had just disappeared."

"So you were going to kill my cat?"

He took a step closer to me. I struggled to keep my eyes on his face and not his glistening six-pack.

"I might have overreacted." He took a deep breath. "Where did you go?"

I crossed my arms over my chest to make sure I didn't do something stupid like run my hands up his flat stomach. "I went to see my best friend. I needed her to know why I ran."

He was studying my face. "She told you there was nothing to forgive?"

"Yeah, something like that."

"Why did you need to tell her? Are you planning on doing something stupid?"

My lips turned up into a smile. "Very. I'm going to join you in the war."

He started to say something, but then he shook his head and sat on the bed. Resting his elbows on his knees, he dropped his head as he leaned forward.

When he didn't say anything, I walked closer to him. "You need me. That's the truth."

"I don't want you to get hurt."

I crouched down and laid my hands on his knees.

Cursing, his head jerked to mine.

"I think," he said, "I know of a way we can win."

My body tensed as a vision swarmed me. Darkness. So much darkness. It was tightly coiled around Evander. A dark power that most fae had only ever heard of but never witnessed until the Winter King. Evander had that same power. I blinked up at him several times.

I chewed my bottom lip. "You'll accept the darkness."

"You've seen me do this?"

My hands tightened on his knees. "Just now."

"I'm assuming it didn't end well?"

I hesitated. "You know that timelines are always changing. If one thing changes, it could change your outcome too, but from what I just saw? No, it didn't end well for you."

He pulled me up from my kneeling position and wrapped his arms around me, laying his head on my shoulder. At first I was shocked, but then I embraced him back. He needed something from me, and I would give him the comfort he sought.

I ran my hand through his hair. "I will do everything I can to work the timelines so that you don't fall into the darkness, but Evander, no one should have this much power."

He nodded against my stomach. His voice was low. "I know."

"If you let the darkness take over you, then we will have a whole new problem. How will we defeat you *and* the king?"

He pulled back from me and tilted up his chin. "If I have to unleash my darkness in order to save everyone, I will do it. Don't worry about me. I'll find a way to not harm anyone."

As visions swirled, his words hit home. It was at that moment that I realized many things. Evander was our only hope of defeating the Winter King. We could hold his army off for a while, but the only way to defeat the king and save humanity was Evander. There was a chance that he would succumb to the darkness that he kept tightly leashed inside of him. But just like that mother that was willing to sacrifice herself to protect her child, Evander would do the same if he thought it would save his friends—if it would save me. I saw it clearly. He was a lot like his mother and nothing like his father. His honey eyes met mine, and he knew that I was fully aware of exactly who he was. The Winter King's biological son.

CHAPTER 23

I WOKE UP EARLY THE NEXT MORNING FEELING ANXIOUS ABOUT THE day's events. By now the guard had told the Winter King that a psychic had freed him. I had a lot to do today, and I had to do it without Evander noticing. Laying there, I stared at the ceiling, feeling so heavy in my thoughts.

I had had many visions in the last twelve hours. They were constantly changing…shifting. I had to stop giving options to the people I cared about. If they had a choice, they could change the timeline. I needed the future to go exactly the way I planned it out. Any difference in the plan would lead to casualties.

In one scenario I saw Charlie's mate dying in order to protect her. If that happened, Charlie would die of a broken heart. Both of them gone. Not acceptable. When altering that timeline, Tandi would fall prey to the hands of demons. She would be dead within the hour. Her mate would go ballistic, and there wouldn't be anything left of the fae village. Innocents would die, and not because of the Winter King. Again unacceptable. So I planned. I changed. I altered. Again someone I loved or considered a friend died. I couldn't sit here and plan the timeline on the least amount of people or loved ones who died. Unacceptable.

There was only one option left. I needed to rattle the Winter King. I needed to get under his skin, and I needed him hyper-focused on Evander and Evander only. If he wasn't focused on saving his army, then we would have a shot of destroying them. In this scenario the only way Evander would win would be if he allowed his darkness to come out and play. I just didn't know if I would be enough to bring him back from the darkness. As hard as I tried to see the future, it was blocked from me. Either fate was being a bitch, or this scenario meant that it was the end of the line for me.

I flung the covers from me and noticed a black tattoo-like design crawling up my hand. I licked my thumb and rubbed it, but it didn't disappear. I took a deep breath and closed my eyes. A vision came to me of Evander standing over me this morning, chanting as he held my hand. He had linked his immortality to me. I had been claimed by a fae prince, just as Ariana had said. As long as he lived, I would live. His death wouldn't affect my longevity, but as long as he breathed, so would I. I would be frozen in time at this age for as many years as the Winter Prince lived. The good news was that he didn't plan on just going into the war, letting his darkness reign, and then just detonating himself. He planned on surviving. The bad news was that he had marked me. Claimed me as his without even asking. I should be livid. Angry. Truth was, I was relieved. This once again would alter the timeline.

After eating a quick breakfast, I found him in the training facility. His warriors were practicing with their powers and their weapons. Vanka gave me a wink as I passed her. I watched as her eyes flicked and then widened when she saw the tattoo on my hand. I grimaced as I marched forward.

I came up behind Evander and could tell without him turning around he knew that I had arrived. His muscles tensed as he gave a sharp command to a young fae throwing a knife at a target.

"Hello, little lamb."

"Turn around, you doofus."

He slowly turned to face me with a smile on his face. "I love it when you call me names."

"Good. I didn't plan on changing that anytime soon." I jerked a thumb to the door. "Can I see you for a moment please."

He sighed but followed me through the warehouse. The whole time he was barking commands at his soldiers. Truth was, this group was as ready as they could get. The rest was up to us. I rubbed my forehead. My friends would show up. I knew this. I just needed to keep all the timelines in order. They had already changed since I started walking to the training facility.

Once we were outdoors, I spun on my heel, facing him. I held up my hand and didn't say a word.

One brow rose as his lips twitched. "You have beautiful skin, little lamb. If that's all you needed to know, I need to get back in there."

I put a hand on his chest, and when his muscles flexed under my palm, I let out a little sigh that made him grin. Jerking my hand away, I remembered that even if I was actually relieved, I couldn't act like it. He would think it was okay to just go around marking people without asking them for permission.

"Did you seriously mark me?"

"Mark you?"

I waved my hand in front of his face.

"Oh," he said, "that."

I rolled my eyes.

"I actually claimed you as my bride. Yes."

I swallowed hard. "Bride?"

"Well when one claims someone, yes that typically means they marked them as their bride."

Hands on hips, I glared at him. "You did it without asking me."

"Fine," he said as he crossed his arms over his chest. "Jolene, will you be my bride?"

"No."

His arms dropped. "What do you mean, no?"

"As crazy as I became, I still knew what that two-letter word meant. Where are you struggling? How can I help? It's kind of hard to talk slower when the word only consists of two letters. What if I put the word 'hell' in front of it? Will that help?" I batted my eyelashes. "Hell no."

He sighed. "You didn't want to leave, remember?"

"I do recall that, yes."

"You are mortal."

"I'm aware of that also."

He ran a hand through his hair. "I'm not letting you stay if you are as fragile as a human."

"I have been doing pretty well."

He didn't say a word.

"So you will remove this as soon as the battle is done?"

"No."

My jaw dropped open. He reached out with one finger and pushed my bottom jaw up, closing my mouth.

"Listen, little lamb," he said as he took a step closer to me. "Once we mark someone as our bride, there is no unmarking them. I've chosen you to be my bride. I can't undo what has been done."

That I didn't expect. This might not be so cut and dry as I once assumed. Now I probably should be truly pissed, and yet once again I couldn't seem to muster up the energy. I looked at the mark on my hand. "Why would you do that?"

He grabbed me by my waist and jerked me toward him. His lips met mine and I melted. Later I would check to see if my flesh was still on my bones. I don't know which one of us was more swept up in the other as his hands tightened around my hips, and my mouth angled to make sure he could take as much as he needed.

Breathless, I broke the kiss. Forgetting momentarily that I was mad at him, I blinked up at him in a daze.

"I claimed you because you are mine. You were always mine. If you weren't so stubborn, you would have already seen that."

His hands dropped slowly, and he turned to walk back into the warehouse. I stood there in the hot sun, my fingers to my lips, wondering if he was right.

Had I recognized that he was actually my mate, but I just didn't want to say it out loud? Ariana had said that my mate would heal me. I sighed as I tipped my head back, letting the sun hit me in my face. Yes, Evander was my mate. Technically he was the Winter King's son. Whether he was crowned or not, he was still a prince.

That's why what I was about to do next was going to be the hardest thing I had ever done. Stepping onto the narrow pathway between the warehouse and some sort of smaller building, I called my shadows to me. The black wisps wrapped around me lovingly before taking me away from here. Away from Evander.

CHAPTER 24

My boots landed in the hall in the Winter King's bedroom. He would be returning from a meeting at any second. I sat down in one of his gaudy chairs near the fireplace in the middle of the room. The purple velvet looked comfortable, but nothing would make this wait more bearable. Thankfully I wouldn't have to wait long.

A multitude of visions had swum through my brain over the past twelve hours, but now I was left with no choice. I would bait the Winter King. Stir the flames and hope that my flippant attitude was enough to provoke the Winter King into acting with his emotions and not his brain. I had always been good at chess, and this would be no different.

The door opened, and the moment the Winter King stepped through, I knew he felt my presence. He didn't look at me as he shut his door and began uncuffing and rolling up his sleeves. I took the time to study him. His features looked so much like Evander, I wondered how no one had put two and two together before now.

His face was strong and handsome. His hair was a lot lighter than Evander's coal black, and it was longer. The wavy strands hit the top of his shoulders. The nose was a tad wider and less perfect, but he was still breathtakingly handsome. It was when his eyes finally met mine that I realized that

Evander must have received his unique eye color from his mother.

"I didn't call for a woman, but if you beg I might make time for you."

What? Eww. No. Hell no. "Yeah, definitely not interested."

His eyes flickered down to my hand. "Interesting."

"Yeah, it's kind of new. Honestly if I was going to get a tattoo, I don't think I would have chosen my hand, only because, you know, with age the hands typically show the years first, but"—I waved my hand at him—"I guess this stops the whole aging process altogether so whatever."

He stood there and blinked at me.

"I'm trying to explain to you how I'm very adaptable. Some would even say easygoing." No one has ever said either of those things about me, but honestly they should.

A vision swarmed me, and I said, "That wouldn't be nice. Besides, for some reason you like this insufferable chair. Lighting me on fire while I'm sitting in it is not a good idea."

He cocked his head to the side. "You read my mind?"

"Psychic."

I felt a power wash over me as my body tensed, and I could feel my power pushing back.

His black brows rose. "You just kept me from entering your mind."

"I kept you from controlling my mind, yes." I crossed my legs. "Again, not nice."

His eyes narrowed. "I've heard of you."

I nodded. "From the guard I released." Another vision flitted to me. "Goodness, you killed him? Again, not nice."

"He shouldn't have been jailed in the first place. He should have killed the ones who put him in the cell."

I shrugged. "Maybe he was being diplomatic. Or maybe he knew that he wouldn't win the fight."

He scoffed. "Xavier was my most powerful guard. That was why I sent him with Alexis."

"You didn't love her, but you wanted her to be protected because she was your favorite mistress." I held up a hand. "And before you ask, I actually did read that thought."

His nose flared in anger over the intrusion. "I'm going to kill you."

I just smiled my crazy smile and hoped it unnerved him.

"Why are you here?"

"Finally," I said, "you ask the right question. I'm here to invite you to the wedding."

He slid his hand to his lower back, and I just continued to smile.

"What wedding?"

"Your son's, silly."

His face paled. "I don't have a son."

"Oh but you do, and can I just say you are going to be so proud. His power is the most powerful in all the fae world." I tapped my lips with my finger pretending to think. "Maybe in the whole world. Close call. But, I digress. Point is you are invited. It's happening tonight at midnight."

"I had planned on visiting No Man's Land anyway."

Pretending to be confused, I scrunched my brow. "Oh, did you? Sorry. Sometimes the switchboard gets a little confusing." I held up a hand, cutting off his next words. "Please hold." After a few seconds I apologized again. "Like I was saying, it's a little crowded up there. What were we talking about? Oh yes, we were discussing you coming to your only child's wedding. Should I mark you down for a plus one?"

He grinned, showing white teeth. "I wouldn't miss it for the world."

My black tendrils enveloped my legs, giving me the distraction that I needed. I disappeared just as he was letting the blade in his hand fly. I smirked as I landed back in No Man's Land. The Winter King had just ruined the despicable chair. I did him a favor. Let's hope he remembered it.

CHAPTER 25

I walked through the cabin, whistling. "Honey, I'm home."

Fatimah lazily opened an eye. "What's happening, sister?"

I sat down next to him and began telling him of my plan. His ears were back as he listened to each minor detail. When I was through, I laid back and closed my eyes. Before he could respond, a vision came to me.

"Oh no," I groaned. "He's back?"

The door swung open, and in walked, um...

Fatimah cleared his throat. "Calhoun, nice to see you again." Then he murmured, "Sniff that lie out, sucker."

"Yes, Calhoun! What are you doing here?"

He ran a hand through his messy blond hair. His clothes were rumpled, and he looked exhausted. "I need that key."

I nodded. "So you've said."

"Do you know where it is?"

Fatimah hissed as Calhoun neared us.

"The key?" I hedged.

"Yes, what else would I be talking about?"

I stood slowly. "I think a lot of people are looking for it. The key is apparently on everyone's Christmas list."

His eyes narrowed. "Is there a reason you're not answering me?"

The door swung open again, this time it was Evander, looking like the sexy beast he was. "Is there a reason that you are on my land? In my cabin? Yelling at my bride?"

"Bride?" Fatimah and Calhoun said at the same time.

Fatimah took in my new tattoo. "Why the hell were you rambling about the end of the world when we have more important matters to discuss?"

Calhoun crossed his arms over his chest. "She's not your bride. She barely remembers her name."

I watched dispassionately as Evander threw Calhoun against a wall. "She is mine, and I thought I told you not to return here."

"Ugh, is this where he makes him go boom?" Fatimah asked. "On another note, if he makes him go boom today, he won't be able to make *me* go boom today." Fatimah shouted, "Kill the pretty boy! Make him look like confetti!"

Calhoun's hands lit up with fire. A week ago, I would have thought that was so badass, but that was before I knew what Evander could do. With an easy smile on his face, Evander took a step toward the fae prince.

"Stop!" I shouted. "I need him."

Evander didn't take his eyes from the fae prince. "You might want to clarify what you mean."

He was jealous. A smile lit my face. "What I meant to say is *we* need him." I took a step toward the two princes. "Calhoun, I give you my word that I will tell you where the key is if you gather your people and meet us here twenty minutes before midnight."

Evander refused to release Calhoun, and by now his face was bright red. "Why?"

"Because we need your help fighting off the winter court. They will come here and try to kill everyone living in the land. You will help us."

Evander dropped Calhoun to his feet.

He glared at me then Evander. "And why would I help the slums?"

"Because if you don't, the Winter King will come after the spring court next, and then your court, then the autumn court. I have seen it. You all either join us or die. After your death, which I saw by the way, the Winter King will continue to the human world. There will be no stopping him. So you either stand with us tonight, or you will die."

"I'm supposed to believe you?"

I shrugged. "Believe what you want. I vow that I speak the truth. You hear my words. Be hidden in the hills twenty minutes past midnight. Give the army from the winter court time to pass by you and your people."

He looked at me in disgust a moment before he glared at Evander. Then he stormed out of the cabin.

"So is he in?" Fatimah asked.

I nodded. "He will be here. He is just mad at the moment. His ego and pride got wounded. He isn't stupid, though."

Evander still looked angry enough to kill someone. His nose was flaring as his eyes took in every inch of me. Tiny thoughts here and there came to me. He was struggling. When a fae claims their fated mate, it makes them act extremely territorial. Coming home to find the one he claimed in a conversation with another male that she used to think of as her mate had made him boil with rage. He was battling with his worry over scaring me and his need to fully claim me.

My face heated.

Knowing the thoughts that I had just caught, he gave me a sexy-as-sin smile.

"Jolene, stay out of my head if you're going to blush over my thoughts." My name rolled off his tongue in a sensual way.

Fatimah groaned. "I'm at war with myself. I want to leave because I'm terrified. I also want to stay because I'm slightly turned on and I don't even know what he was thinking."

The door opened wide, and Evander said, "Out."

I watched as my pet demon hopped down and grumbled the whole way out the door.

By the time the door had closed, Evander had advanced on me. He snagged me by my branded hand, pulling me hard into his chest. My arms went around his neck as his lips pressed against mine. His lips trailed from my mouth down my neck as he muttered against my skin, "You should probably stay out of my head right now."

I half-moaned and half-laughed. "Now I'm really intrigued."

His lips made their way back to mine. He gave me one more kiss before he lightly pulled away and rested his forehead against mine.

"Tell me, little lamb, is the war to begin at midnight?"

I breathed in the scent of him and almost sighed. "Yes, that's the specific time I invited the Winter King to come."

His whole body stiffened against me. "What do you mean?"

"I invited your father to a wedding. Ours, to be exact."

He took a step back from me. "You went to see the Winter King?"

"I know you are about to explode so let me explain. Every scenario I have seen ends with someone I love dying. This is the only scenario where we have a chance of making it through this without losing someone. Before you storm off and waste the rest of the day being mad at me, know that this is how it had to be."

His chest raised and fell slowly for a few moments before he said, "Tell me everything."

"I had no other option but to see him. It will give everyone their best chance at surviving the upcoming war."

"And what was the purpose?"

I knew he would get mad at my next words. "To goad him."

I was right. He said a few choice words and paced the floor in front of me. When he finally calmed down, I said, "We need him hyper-focused on certain things. I can't tell you any more or it'll change the timelines."

I thought he would argue, but he gave me a curt nod. "I don't like it, but I understand."

I looked at my tattoo and then back at him. "If I could have ended him, I would have, but the only person that will be able to get close enough to the Winter King to strike him down is you. Unless his attention is elsewhere." I scrunched up my nose as a vision came to me. "Rest assured if he is caught unaware, I will help you end him." I could tell he was about to ask more questions that I couldn't answer. "Do you want to go for a walk?"

I wasn't as smooth as I thought I was. He gave me a sexy smile. "I understand. How would you like to spend the rest of the day?"

I looked down at the floor, before finally dragging my gaze up to his. "Getting to know my, um…"

"Mate," he grinned.

I nodded.

He held out his hand. "Come then. I'll take you through the forest where we can talk."

Frowning, I said, "We can't talk here?"

He walked quietly to the door and shook his head. When he opened it, the cat stumbled through. "Not with the demon listening to every word."

Fatimah bolted into the room and hid under the kitchen table. I was laughing as I exited the cabin with Evander. Tonight we would have the biggest battle that would take place for at least a century. There were so many timelines blurring in front of me. I probably needed to rest, but what if the timeline changed again? I needed to be awake for it.

I needed to stay awake, and I needed to enjoy this moment here and now with my mate. If this was to be my last day on this earth, there is no one I'd rather spend it with than the man who looks at me like I'm the most precious being in the world.

CHAPTER 26

On our way back to the cabin, I asked him if we could stop by the village. His golden eyes searched my face as his hand tightened on mine.

"What do you have planned, little lamb?"

I beamed up at him. "I want to introduce you to my friends. They have just arrived." I let a vision roll right through me and tried not to sigh. The damn timelines just changed again. Keeping so many people on the right track was going to be the end of me. "Sorry," I said, "what I was saying is my friends are here and I need to talk with them." Death in particular, if the stubborn male would listen.

As we rounded the corner, Evander pulled me behind him as he let out a shout. I ran around him, ignoring his curses and running toward the huge ogre in front of the little pub. He was massive in size and was one hundred percent the reason that the streets were cleared.

"Kong!" I said affectionately as I threw my arms around the ogre's kneecaps because that's how tall he was. "I have missed you so much."

He patted my head, and I swear something in my spine cracked. "Jo, my friend."

"Aww thanks, bud. Is the rest of the gang inside?"

Again he patted me on the head, and I winced. "Yes, friend."

With one more squeeze I let him go. "See you soon, big guy."

Evander never once took his eyes from the ogre as he went past him. He grabbed my elbow lightly. "As I said, you get more and more interesting."

I giggled like the end of the world wasn't upon us and pushed open the pub doors. The bar was spacious, but all the beings packed inside made it look small. I took them all in at once. CG was leaning up against the bar. Sadie's hand was in his, and they looked like they were having a serious conversation. From the fleeting thoughts of the shifter, I could tell he was worried about his mate. He didn't want her in this battle, but he also knew that he couldn't force her to leave.

His brother was sitting in a chair on the opposite side of the room. CG had a dark, stoic look to him. Jamison was the other side of the coin. He had an angelic appearance, and he was all smiles, especially since his mate Charlie was sitting on his lap. She was dipping her fingers in a cup, flinging the droplets, and freezing them mid-air before they hit the table.

Carmen was throwing darts at a picture on the wall. Austin stood beside her, shaking his head as he grinned at her lack of cussing.

"Duck's sake!" she said. "How did I miss?" Her glossy, black hair swung over one shoulder as she narrowed her dark eyes and threw another dart. Austin, with his white-blonde hair and cool gaze, looked the complete opposite of her dark-haired beauty, and yet they fit so perfectly together.

Death stood in the corner, looking sexy as ever. His brown eyes immediately fell on me the moment I stepped over the threshold. I used to think that Death shouldn't be so sexy, but I guess if you were in your last moments, you would want someone as hot as him escorting you to the other side of the veil. Tamara, the red-headed Zombie Queen—and also his mate—put her hands over her belly and gave me a wink. I smiled in return. She was pregnant and there were only three people in this room who knew. I would keep their secret until they were ready to share it with the others.

Sasha and Kian were twirling around to music that only existed in their heads. The childhood friends and mates both had similar coloring. Sasha's face was pure delight as the king of the sea dipped his lover. She was laughing like the end of the world wasn't at our doorstep, and that made my heart feel lighter.

Tandi and Stephan were kissing each other like we were about to go to war and might never see one another again. The sexy vampire threaded his fingers through his mate's long, blonde hair and then skimmed her sides like he knew every dip and curve she had. She pulled away from him, and then whispered something in his ear, causing him to growl and her to laugh.

I blinked the tears away as I took in each of their faces. They were my family. I couldn't lose a single person here.

They were now all looking at me and studying Evander. He stood by my side as Sadie ran up to me and gave me a hug.

"We're on time, right?" she asked.

I nodded. "Yep." She stood to my side as I addressed everyone. "Hey, fam. Miss me?"

There was laughter and cheers as each of the twelve people came up to me and gave me a hug. After all their questions were answered, I stood to the side. "This is Evander."

Sadie was the first one to speak. "Nice to meet you." I caught her thoughts and laughed. She was thinking she understood why I was having problems with my fae prince mate if this gorgeous male was by my side.

"Yeah, turns out Calhoun isn't my mate."

"You read my mind?"

I nodded.

"Holy shit."

Evander took that moment to say, "I'm her mate."

Carmen whistled and Austin glared at her, which only made her laugh. "Hey, there's only one man for me, buddy."

I clapped my hands to get everyone to focus, which was hilarious because it was usually *me* who had a hard time concentrating. "Okay everyone, here this is what I need from you. The summer court will be on the hill above the villages. They must come in late, or the Winter King will see them. I need all of you to hold off as much of the king's army as you can until I get back."

Charlie's blue eyes flickered to mine. "Get back? Where are you going?"

"Sorry, can't say. It'll change the timelines."

Carmen picked up her discarded leather jacket and put it back on. "So we need to hold off how many?"

"Just ten thousand," Death answered as he produced his scythe from nowhere. "No biggie."

CG said, "We brought our shifters. They are in the first village."

Jamison added, "Hopefully the war will start soon. I think they are making everyone nervous."

"That's why I put my demons in the forest," Carmen said. "Plus I didn't want them eating everyone."

"Yeah," I said. "Good call. We don't need demons eating the fae kids. It's bad for business."

"If I have your permission," Tamara said, "I will call forth all those buried in these grounds."

I nodded. "Yes, that sounds good. There aren't many, but it's enough to slow them down."

"You've already seen all of this, haven't you?" asked Tandi.

"Yeah, but some of you keep changing the timelines. It's super annoying." I shook my head. "Okay that's the plan. Hold them off until we're back. You'll think you're losing, but if no one panics" —my eyes flickered over to Death—"then we will be fine."

I gave everyone goodbye hugs and then went over to Death. "I need to talk to you alone for a second."

Tamara looked over at us nervously but didn't intervene when Death followed me outside. Evander had come out of the pub, but he gave us a wide berth. He was looking around for Kong, who had disappeared. He had a frown on his sexy face, and I could feel his worry so I said, "Kong is a vegetarian."

If I thought that would make him feel better, it didn't. He walked a little ways to look down the alleys.

I gave all my attention to Death, knowing he was worried and wanted something from me. He needed to know that his mate was going to be fine. "I know you're nervous about letting the mother of your unborn child fight in a war."

He clenched his jaw, and his eyes darted to the pub before landing on me. "What do you have for me, soothsayer?"

"She will get wounded."

His eyes blazed and fists clenched.

"Easy," I said. "I'm telling you this because I trust you. If you try to stop her from getting wounded, the timeline changes and I will lose three of the people who are in that pub. Her wound will be superficial. She'll heal before she leaves this place. The baby will be fine. Do not worry about her. Do not try to keep her in your sights. Your mate is strong. She will be fine as long as you carry your weight. You can't do that if you're constantly looking over her shoulder."

He nodded. "I hear you. I'll let my more-than-capable mate fight her own battles."

"Then we all might survive this."

Without saying another word, he strode purposefully straight to the pub—and his mate. I sighed and my shoulders drooped as a vision came to me. After my talk with Death, this vision was better. It was one I could live with.

Evander cleared his throat. "You want to go get ready?"

"Ready?" I asked with a frown.

He closed the distance between us and leaned toward me, his lips descending on mine. I could feel his desperation and his worry in the kiss. He didn't think he would survive the darkness if he had to let it reign.

I tried to ease his worry by letting my body do the talking. My hands roamed his chest, lingering a second over his heart before traveling up his shoulders. He parted my lips and gave me the most heated kiss I had ever received. Warmth spread in my belly as I tried to somehow get closer to him. He walked me backward until my back hit the outside of the pub. His knee went in between my legs, and I thought I was going to burst. He pulled back slightly. His chest was heaving and I was staring up at him wide-eyed as the aftermath of the kiss still pulsed through my body.

Smirking, he rubbed his thumb over my swollen lip. "Yes, do you want to go get ready?"

I blinked more times than necessary but holy hell that was a kiss I'd never forget. "Ready for what?"

"Our wedding."

I was having a hard time forming words, so I just nodded. I mean the wedding was a lure to get the Winter King to come two days earlier than he planned. I wanted him a little less organized, and I wanted his wrath on Evander instead of hyper-focused on killing our army. If his attention was divided, we would be able to take him out more easily. It also gave our army a chance because here was the bad news that I didn't want to tell anyone: The Winter King had a darkness inside of him, too. He ruled with it daily. If he let out his darkness on the army, we didn't have a chance. We would all be dead within the hour.

No, he needed to focus on the one person who could match his darkness.

I just prayed that Evander enjoyed that kiss enough for it to help anchor him to me. That he remembered there were people here counting on him. If he let the darkness rule him, it would be like turning off his humanity, and I would be nothing to him, mate or not.

CHAPTER 27

AFTER MEETING WITH MY FRIENDS, I SHOULD HAVE FELT A CERTAIN amount of peace in my heart, but all I felt was worry. My anxiety was at an all-time high. I knew that whatever happened tonight, I should know that I tried my best to protect all those whom I loved, but that wasn't my personality. I would take any mistake as a complete failure.

Evander dropped me off at the cabin and told me he would meet me by the waterfall before midnight. I was hoping for one more of those earth-shattering kisses, but it never came. I walked into the quiet cabin with so much on my mind that at first I didn't even see the box that Evander had left on the bed.

When I opened it, I almost cried. The most beautiful wedding gown lay inside. It was silly to get choked up. I had said we were having a wedding to bait the Winter King, but the fact that he went out of his way to make a farce wedding special made me crush on the hot villain even more. Another vision came while I was putting on the gown. I sighed in relief. We were right on track.

Shay and Vanka had come by to escort me to the waterfall. They looked fierce in their warrior paint. I patted Vanka on the hand. I knew that she would take a blade to the stomach in less than an hour. It would hurt like hell. She would heal, though, and if I told her to dodge the blade, then she would be so worried about what was to come that she wouldn't be focused. If her concentration was broken, it would cost her her life. So I just kept my mouth shut.

My cat solemnly walked beside us along the trail. I think he was more stressed about the upcoming battle than I was.

"We are all going to die," Fatimah said.

"Neither of us knows that."

"Well," he hissed, "now would be a good time to figure things out. I mean, what's the point of having all these visions if you can't even tell me if we live past this night?"

"Don't be so crabby. Just because I don't know doesn't mean you will die. If no one deviates from what I need them to do, then we will be fine."

"Oh great," the cat said. "Someone sneezes early and we're all dead."

I snorted. "You can go hide in the cabin."

His fur ruffled and he stopped walking. "Are you kidding me? I would never leave my master to die alone. Now if you'll excuse me, I'm going to go get a good seat."

I shook my head as I walked up the trail to the waterfall. I saw Evander standing on the same flat rock where he taught me to open up my powers. He looked so handsome in his military attire of fitted black cargo pants and T-shirt. I was a little overdressed, but I didn't care.

"You look beautiful," he said as I neared him.

"Thank you."

His eyes took in the scenery ahead of us. "Are you sure about this?"

I nodded. "Very."

He went up ahead of me to scout the area. I couldn't hear the Winter King marching this way, but he would be here in minutes. The waterfall was on the boundary of the summer court. They would pass by Calhoun and the few soldiers he was able to beg for help. With all our numbers, we were still six to ten. Not great odds, but doable.

I stood facing Evander. I put my hands on my hips. His eyes went to the mark on my hand.

"Why midnight?" he asked.

"It's when you are at your strongest." I reached up and gave him a kiss. "I'll see you in a few minutes."

He cocked his head to the side. "What do you mean? Where are you going?"

I would not cry. I looked into his eyes and whispered, "I said we were baiting him. You're the bait." My wisps of shadows carried me from the waterfall, but not before I saw the look of betrayal on his face or the shouts of the king's army.

CHAPTER 28

THIS WOULD BE THE HARDEST PART FOR ME. SITTING IN A TREE AND watching. I could swear that Evander could still somehow feel me. His eyes kept flickering up to my hiding spot. His shoulders were thrust back as the Winter King came marching toward him. I could feel his army spreading out through the forest. When he came into view, he stopped twenty feet from Evander, who turned away from my hiding spot and faced his father. Hands in pockets, he cocked his head to the side and just waited.

The Winter King sneered as his eyes traveled the length of Evander. "So, you're my son?"

Evander laughed. "Don't call me that."

"I assumed that you were dead."

"Oh, when you carried out that child massacre in the villages? Sorry to disappoint."

The king snarled, "I'll remedy that soon enough. Don't worry."

I felt his power rumbling from him as a vision came to me. The summer court had started picking off as many of the army as they could with bows and arrows. They wouldn't leave their high spots. They lacked bravery, but at least they had shown up. When the army started to pursue them, they were to run down the backside of their hills and enter the village. They'd lead them to my friends, who would be waiting. We wanted the king separated from his army. If he was pulling their strings, we didn't stand a chance.

Power rumbled from the Winter King as he flung his arms wide. He was trying to kill Evander without touching him. He wanted him in pieces. Literally. Just like what Evander had done to Alexis. Evander's power rumbled from him as a protection from his father's attack. I smiled as the Winter King's power bounced off Evander. Thanks to the many visions that had been streaming in, I knew that—like his son—the Winter King could only pull that trick once and it was spent. He wouldn't be able to get enough energy up for at least twenty-four hours.

But we couldn't have Evander wasting his power like his father did. So that was my cue. I let my shadows carry me right in front of the Winter King, just as twenty of his armed men came rushing through the forest. They were here to tell the king he was under attacked from the summer court.

I interrupted them with a wave to the Winter King. "Hey! Remember me? I'm the one who hated your tacky furniture."

He was speechless. Didn't blame him. I sort of had that effect on people. I leaned in close and whispered, "This is where you kidnap me, silly."

His mouth dropped open and closed as Evander shouted, probably envisioning his father melting the flesh from my bones. But he couldn't see what I saw. No, the Winter King wanted to make sure that the one person who could take him down was dead. He couldn't do that unless his son was weak. I felt Evander's thoughts being pushed at me.

"You said I was the bait."

I looked over at him. *"You are."*

Cold hands grabbed me around the waist. I could feel Evander's power ramping up. Before we disappeared, I yelled, "Save it, big guy!" And then, just like that, we were gone.

Moments later, we landed in a windowless basement. I sighed as I instantly recognized where I was.

"Love what you have done with the place," I said. "That smell, is it mold?"

"I will kill you slowly after I'm done with my son." He shoved me into a cell and left the same way he came. I rolled my eyes and sat in the nasty corner, waiting for death.

CHAPTER 29

OF COURSE EVANDER ALLOWED THEM TO DRAG HIM HERE. HIS mate was here. He was spitting mad at the king. At me. At the world. I could hear his thoughts because he wanted me to hear them.

"Little lamb, when we get out of this, I'm going to spank you."

Promises, promises, I thought to myself.

I thought I would be ready for the next part, but in reality, I wasn't. Not by a long shot.

I could hear the guards taunting Evander. They had chained him to the wall. My stomach roiled at the thought of the pain he was about to endure. I could hear the Winter King dismissing them. I could feel Evander's pain when the Winter King started to melt parts of his flesh from his body. I was so close to them that I could smell the flesh, and the stench caught in my throat, making my eyes water.

Another vision came to me, and the timeline changed. Damn, Death. Did I not tell him to not worry about his mate? I stood up and started to pace. Why would no one listen to me? If we all survived this, I was going to kill the grim reaper.

Five freaking devastating minutes later, Death shows up.

"Where the hell have you been?" I hissed.

He extracted a key from his pocket and released me from my cell. "Making sure my mate was fine."

"I told you she would be."

There was a sound above us. "I'm guessing the other guards found the ones I beheaded to get that key. Do you need my services?"

"Um yeah, go kill all the ones running this way, and stop changing my timelines, asshole."

He gave me a smirk before disappearing.

I ran the length of the cells, counting them in my head. My nighttime vision was crap. When I got to cell number fourteen, I stopped. There was a little light inside the cell. I could see Evander sitting on the floor, his wrists encircled with cuffs and his arms shackled above his head. With the iron cuffs on, he was completely harmless. The king knew this and was overconfident. This is the part where Evander would have to use his darkness, and I would pray he would be able to rein it in.

The king was standing over Evander sneering with resentment. "Tell me where the key is."

"I'm waiting," Evander said as he tilted his head back to glare at his father. Blood trickled out of his mouth, and I once again cursed Death and his lateness. People who say Death is always on time never met the asshole.

"What are you waiting for?" the king asked, sounding genuinely intrigued.

"Distraction."

I cleared my throat, and the Winter King whirled. It was in that brief moment that his power slipped. He was no longer focused on protecting himself against his son. I saw the moment he realized what his son had meant. His powers swirled but it was too late. I jumped to the side just in time to see pieces of the Winter King fly through the bars. I gagged as Evander growled.

"Just a second," I said. "I didn't realize that I had a weak stomach." I closed my eyes as I stepped over the pieces of the king. "So, not the wedding I had envisioned." Then I laughed as I opened Evander's cell. "Just kidding. This is exactly how I pictured it."

I stood in front of the doors and watched as Evander jerked the chains from the wall. He made it to his feet, and I watched in equal parts fascination and horror as the cuffs melted from his wrists. It was badass and scary all at the same time.

"Evander," I cooed. "I'm going to need you to rein that darkness back in."

He marched to the door and grabbed a hold of the iron bars. His hands sizzled but he didn't even flinch as he pried the bars from one another with an unfathomable strength.

"I had a key," I whispered as he stepped through the opening. As hard as I tried, I never received a vision of what happened after Evander let his darkness free. I swallowed nervously. Maybe this is where I died? His nostrils flared as the gold in his eyes swirled. He was out of control. At least the Winter King's darkness wouldn't be able to wash over Evander's soldiers and my friends. That was one thing they wouldn't have to worry about.

He took a step toward me. I put a hand on his chest like I could stop him. "Please don't melt my flesh from my bones. Remember how you said I had pretty skin? You seemed to like it. You also don't like to waste things, remember?"

Please remember. He cocked his head to the side. I couldn't pick up on any of his thoughts. It was as if his humanity had been completely shut off.

"Please," I begged.

He didn't move as I nervously wrapped my arms around his neck and stood on my tiptoes. I was still too far away from his lips, and he wasn't dipping his head to meet mine. Trying to avoid the missing patches of flesh, I threw my legs around his waist and climbed up him, holding tight. I looked into his unblinking eyes. He hadn't melted me yet. That had to be a good sign. I trailed kisses along his jawline and felt him stiffen. My lips grazed his, but he was like a statue under my hold. I delicately ran my tongue over his bottom lip, trying to get some warmth back into him. My legs tightened around him as I nibbled at his mouth. Finally, his arms came around me and I almost sighed with relief. His lips aggressively attacked mine, and I let him kiss me. I felt him thawing under me with every flick and swipe of his tongue. What seemed like hours was only minutes when he finally stood me on my feet.

He rested his forehead against mine and cradled my face in his large hands. "Thank you, little lamb."

I was too emotional to do more than nod.

We stood there, soaking in our feelings for one another.

Finally he said, "We need to go and help the others."

"Yes, we do."

He wrapped his arms around me. "I'll take you."

As we moved from the winter court, all I could do was think how thankful I was. This wasn't over, but Evander had won his battle. He had let the darkness inside him out to play and he had reined it in. I had felt his thoughts when he was kissing me, so I knew the only reason he was able to come back to himself was because of me. Right then I vowed to always be his anchor in the storm.

CHAPTER 30

WE ARRIVED IN THE THICK OF THE BATTLE. THE SUMMER COURT had dared to venture close, but not close enough that they couldn't run if needed. CG and Jamison, along with their shifters, tore into the late Winter King's guards like they were chew toys. Austin went through a crowd of enemy shifters. His blade swung so fast I hardly saw the weapon.

I shoved Evander to the right. "Go. Tandi needs your help."

"What about you?"

"Oh, I'll be fine." I disappeared into my shadows so he wouldn't argue with me. Stubborn man.

I reappeared farther in the middle of the fighting. Stephan was flashing from one spot to the next, ripping throats out with his bloody fangs. He was having the time of his life. I shook my head as I disappeared again.

I landed five feet from Death and chuckled. My body felt weird. Sadie had just frozen time. Obviously not for long, because we were still on the right track. Ice was thrown like daggers into a horde of demons. I couldn't see Charlie's small frame, but I knew that she was the wielder. Death disappeared from view as eight heads rolled to my feet. The man was quick.

Carmen was riding a black panther as she came trotting through the battle. She gave me a wink as she ran a blade through a witch from the king's army. I heard a chuckle from the panther that I recognized as Fatimah's.

She gave me a grin. "I fixed your pet. Hope you don't mind."

Fatimah said, "Bigger is better, right, Jo?"

I shook my head at the both of them as they continued through the throng of enemies. They were both making jokes as they brought the king's army to their knees. Kian and Sasha were fighting like they were joined at the hip. One would slash and the other would stab. It was a beautiful thing to watch. They knew exactly how each other fought and it amplified their own skills. They moved like trained dancers who had practiced for hours to perform the most hypnotic choreography I had ever witnessed.

I caught an arrow before it had a chance to penetrate my left eye. A male fae was headed my way, a murderous look on his face.

"That wasn't very nice." He restrung his bow, and I rolled my eyes. "Dude, why bother? You're dead anyway."

He arched a brow just as Tandi came up behind him and twisted his neck. She winced and apologized to the fallen fae. She gave me a weak smile. "I really loathe killing. I'm going to need buckets of therapy after this."

I nodded. "Duck."

Without hesitation, she dropped to the ground. The fireball thrown her way fell over her and landed on one of Carmen's demons, who didn't even feel the flame. Tandi slowly got to her feet.

"I'm going to kill that witch," she said as she took off at a dead run.

I was glad to see she was working through her problems.

I disappeared right on time. Stupid shifter was about to pounce. I reappeared at the edge of the battle. I watched as bones and skeletons began to march through the crowd. Tamara stood at the edge of the battlefield. Her blue eyes swirled with mischief as her creations joined the fray. She had a cut on her shoulder, and even though she would be fine, it still worried me.

She caught me staring. "Hey, crazy!" she yelled. "Quit giving me that look. I'm preggers, not dying." Then her eyes widened. "I'm not dying, am I?"

I shook my head with a smile. "Nope."

I moved once again. This time to go check on Evander. He was between Shay and Vanka, with Kong at their back. The huge ogre was throwing demons like bowling balls and laughing when they went crashing into the enemy. He was so cute.

Evander was wielding his sword like he had been born with it. The king might have only been able to take sections of flesh from a person, but my honey could melt the whole epidermis. If anyone got to close, he would just reach out and boom. They melted. He was such a badass. I ducked as two shifters threw a punch over my head. Moving so that I was away from their little skirmish, I continued to watch Evander fight. There was such a quickness to his blade that bodies were falling before I could blink.

Carmen came riding up on Fatimah. She had a beer in one hand and a sword in the other. When did she have time to grab a beer?

I pinched the bridge of my nose. A male vampire was about to swing an ax at my head. My plan was to do my disappearing act, but a vision came to me, making me freeze. Evander's eyes widened in horror a moment before pieces of flesh from some poor soul hit my skin. I looked over at Carmen. Her face was pale, and her dark eyes were rounded in shock. She chucked her beer at a nearby witch without looking at her.

"Did he just…" she said.

Fatimah answered, "Yep."

Shay and Vanka picked up the slack as Evander ignored everyone around him. "What just happened? Why didn't you disappear?"

He was angry as he approached me.

I yelled back, "I tried but I got a vision! It threw me off for a second."

Still shouting, he said, "You are going to have to get better at receiving them. That vampire almost killed you."

"Yeah, well now I'm wearing him!" I flicked a piece of flesh off my arm. If I had ever been right in the head, which was highly unlikely, there would be no hope for me again in the future.

He pulled me toward him, and I hit his chest. I could see

Carmen swinging her blade at an approaching witch while the large panther swiped the leg of a fae male who dared to get too close.

"How did you just do that, anyway?" I asked. "I thought you could only, um…"

"Make people turn into confetti," Fatimah supplied.

"Yeah, what he said."

Evander shook his head. "I thought I could do it only once, as well, but I guess when you really want something you can make it happen twice in a row."

Fatimah whistled. "Do you hear what they are talking about, Carmen? It's getting so kinky over there. Like I'm getting all hot and bothered."

Evander stabbed someone behind me without blinking. "I hate that cat."

"Can I have him then?" Carmen asked sweetly. "He is such a good boy."

"No," I said as Evander said, "Yes."

Carmen giggled. "Come on, Fatimah, let's see if, um…he can go a third round."

"They are so immature," I said. "I love it."

Shay yelled, "A little help over here, sir!"

Evander grabbed me by my shirt and jerked me toward him. "Be safe. If you feel a vision coming on, go and prepare to take flight to anywhere but here. Do you understand me?"

"Yes, I'll go poof next time."

He gave me a quick kiss and went back to help Shay. I disappeared to where I was needed. Jamison was looking for Charlie, but she was more than fine. He needed to watch the four demons that were creeping up on him.

For the next four and half hours, I kept bouncing around, giving words of encouragement and making sure they ducked, dodged, and moved when I told them to. I was freaking exhausted, but we were keeping on our timelines. That's all that mattered.

CHAPTER 31

THE SUN WAS PEEKING UP OVER THE HORIZON, AND WE WERE ALL sitting in a bar. I was covered in chunks of flesh, and my hair was matted with blood. Not mine. Kian had hit a major artery on an approaching fae, and I dared to get too close. I was drenched.

I looked at everyone laughing and smiling. Charlie kept running out of the pub to bring Kong more food and water. The ogre couldn't fit inside of the bar. Not without taking the roof off.

This was my family. I looked over to where Death was sitting up against a wall. Tamara's head was in his lap, and she was sound asleep.

A vision hit me so hard that I shook.

The woman who I saved the day my granny died was delivering her child today. That little boy would grow up and search for his mate. My trembling fingers touched my lips. The baby that Tamara carried would be the mate of the child that was being born today. If they found one another, they would protect us in the next battle that was to take place.

Fate stepped in that day and changed the lives of all of us. I wish it would have allowed me to save my granny, but the choice was taken from me. Truth was, if I hadn't been broken by her death, would I have ever come here to be fixed? Would I have ever met Evander? Would the Winter King have destroyed everything in No Man's Land and then gone to our world to take each one of us out while we were divided? Did granny's death bring us to this moment? To victory? I believed so.

"Are you okay?" Evander asked as he handed me a cold drink. I winced when I saw it was the same nasty beer that I had tried in this same pub not too long ago. "You look like you are about to cry."

"No, I'm good," I replied, taking the mug from him. "Just thankful for my granny. That's all."

He gave me a kiss on top of my head, and my nose wrinkled. "I cannot believe you just did that."

"I don't mind a little blood."

I shook my head in disgust. "Well, that makes one of us. I need a shower."

He took my mug from me and sat it on a nearby table. "Tell your friends goodbye."

"Now?"

He helped me to my feet. "Well, it is our honeymoon."

Before I could utter a word, he had me wrapped in his arms and back in his cabin. He pushed me toward the shower, and once my body was scrubbed clean and I had put on some clothes, he took his own shower. When he came out in only a towel, my nerves got the best of me and my mouth started running.

Jokingly, I said, "You better hope that Fatimah doesn't come bursting through the door at any moment."

He gave me a slow, sizzling smile that I felt all the way to my toes. "I've already ensured that we would have complete privacy. I can promise you that we don't have to worry about your demon tonight."

He stalked toward me like I was his prey, and I swallowed. My shyness was overcoming me, and I could feel my face heating. He reached out and ran the back of his hand down my cheek. I felt out of my element and prayed that whatever happened next wouldn't be a fumbling, awkward mess.

As if *he* was the mind reader, he smiled lovingly at me. "You could never be anything less than perfect, Jolene."

He pulled my body against his, and the towel dropped. My eyes widened. He smirked. "What, you didn't see this happening?"

I shook my head. I was glad that I had no visions of this. I wanted to experience it like it truly was the first time. My eyes swept over his bare chest, taking in all the tattoos that made him even more sinfully delicious. My mind tried to burn the images of his rock-hard pecs into my frontal lobe. It was something that I'd want to pull up and remember over and over. My eyes jerked back to his before I could see too much. Evander laughed as he dipped his head to mine. My arms wrapped around his waist as he devoured me. He picked me up and carried me to his bed, and I realized that maybe I was the doomsayer queen, the prophet of doom, the 'hell is upon your doorstep' girl. I was also the chick that could give everyone hope for a better tomorrow. Well, as long as they stayed on my timelines.

My thoughts escaped me as I lay on the bed and he trailed a series of kisses down my throat and over my collarbone. This might not be heaven, but it was close. The best part was that we would live to do this again and again. How could I possibly want for more?

ACKNOWLEDGMENTS

First I have to give thanks to God for helping me to do what I love. Thanks to my editor Susan with Readers Cave, Martha Ashe, Donna Augustine, and Pam Luna for taking the time to read this book. Thanks to Michelle Fritz because you're awesome! SA Soule thank you for formatting. Additional thanks to Molly for the cover.

To my village- I love each of you and would be lost and miserable without your beautiful faces. You each make life bearable and more fun. Happy Birthday Caity!

Thank you to the readers who have been by my side since day one. All of you keep me going. Last but not least, thank you to my family. You guys keep me going.

ABOUT THE AUTHOR

Brandi Elledge lives in the South, where even the simplest words have at least four syllables.

She has a husband that she refuses to upgrade...because let's face it he is pretty awesome, and two beautiful children that are the light of her life.

https://brandielledge.com

Join Brandi's super fans on her Facebook Group at Brandi's Book Mavens. There are always giveaways! Who doesn't like free stuff? https://www.facebook.com/groups/264139701188022/

Sign up to my newsletter to be the first to hear about each new book in the series. https://sendfox.com/elite.dance

Made in United States
North Haven, CT
07 January 2024

47140464R00124